SOMEBODY
TO LOVE

SOMEBODY
TO LOVE

•

Roni Denholtz

AVALON BOOKS
NEW YORK

PRINTED IN THE UNITED STATES OF AMERICA
ON ACID-FREE PAPER
BY HADDON CRAFTSMEN, BLOOMSBURG, PENNSYLVANIA

For my children
Amy Lynelle & Joshua Max
Who always told me I would succeed . . .
and who share my love of music

AND

for all the brave policemen, firefighters and
rescue workers, human and canine,
who worked round the clock on 9/11:
and for the journalists who tirelessly covered the events

ACKNOWLEDGMENTS

With thanks to Russ Long, Deirdre Bryant, Norm Worth and all of the staff at WRNJ, 1510 AM, Hackettstown—Washington. They answered tons of questions for my background research and gave me the opportunity to go on the air. And they provide the music I love to listen to whether I'm working at the computer or driving in my car!

Chapter One

W ho was this man, and what was he doing at the radio station?

Grace paused in the act of leading the Brownie troop out of the studio. She couldn't help staring.

The man who stood at the end of the hall, a sheaf of papers in his hand, was well over six feet. Broad-shouldered, with light-brown hair, he looked like he was in his late twenties. He was one of the handsomest men she'd encountered in a long time.

But that wasn't why she was feeling such a jolt to her senses. No, it was something else about him. An air of quiet command and capability surrounded him, the kind of aura that made people sit up with respect and listen.

Grace felt her heart ping as the stranger met her gaze head-on.

He wore a navy suit and stylish glasses. As he studied her, Grace exhaled in a long sigh and realized she'd been holding her breath.

"Who's that?"

One of the Brownies pointed at the unknown man.

Behind the stranger, Mr. Armstrong, the station's owner and manager, rounded the corner.

"Uh, Grace . . . ?" It was the voice of Paulette Nichols, one

1

of the mothers accompanying the troop on their tour of the radio station.

Grace snapped back to attention. She had to refocus on the troop, and finish up the tour she was giving them. Later she could ponder the fact that this man was eliciting a strong reaction within her. A reaction that made her feel like a guitar string that was plucked and set vibrating.

Grace swallowed. "I don't know who that is," she answered the young girl's question. "But the other man behind him is Charles Armstrong, the owner and manager of radio station WQNJ."

Charles Armstrong stepped forward, smiling at the girls. "Hello there. Glad you could see the station," he greeted them. "I hope you enjoyed the tour." His jovial face, framed by thick white hair, beamed at the group.

He was answered by a chorus of yeses. He turned to Grace.

"Grace, you haven't had a chance to meet our new advertising and events director. This is Brian Talbot. Brian, Grace Norwood. Also known as Grace Harmony, our late-afternoon DJ."

Brain Talbot took a step toward her. Grace extended her hand, feeling smaller and fragile in comparison to his height. His hand, large and masculine, was warm and strong as it grasped hers.

"I've heard a lot of good things about you," he said. His voice was deep and the timbre was friendly and pleasing.

So this was the new ad director! Grace knew he'd started this past Monday, but he was usually out on the road by the time she arrived at the station. She had to agree silently with Tina, the secretary, who'd called Brian "hot."

She gave him a bright smile and stepped back, freeing her hand. The warm feeling inside her remained.

"I've heard good things about you too," Grace responded, smiling. "I'm glad to meet you. Welcome to WQNJ. You're going to love it here."

Where his hand held hers Grace felt as if vibrations were

humming and then traveling up her arm and through her entire being. Her heart skipped along with the music.

Brian was giving her an appraising look, and Grace suddenly felt self-conscious. It was a feeling she rarely experienced.

Why did the man of her dreams have to walk into her life when she looked like an eighteen-year-old?

Of course, she knew she couldn't tell from his outer appearance if this man really was the stuff that dreams are made of. But he certainly looked the part.

While she looked like a young hippie.

To go along with her radio show at the oldies station she usually dressed in clothes that were similar to the styles of the late '60s and early '70s. But Grace found herself wishing she hadn't selected her long, tie-dyed pink and purple T-shirt to wear over a white turtleneck top with her faded pair of jeans. For just a moment, she wished she was wearing a simple business suit. Or a feminine dress. And that her hair wasn't pulled back in a scrunchie.

She had to bring her scattered thoughts together. She still had the Brownie troop to consider, and soon it would be time to go on the air.

"Grace Harmony?" He repeated Charles's words, emphasizing the Harmony.

"It's my middle name," she explained hastily. She was used to people's surprised reactions, and had even told the troop about her family's unique names.

"She's named for a famous rock and roll singer." The solemn voice came from LaShone Nichols, Grace's personal "little sister" from the Big Sisters program. "She told us her mom liked the singer's voice a lot."

Grace caught a hint of amusement in Brian's hazel eyes as he smiled at the Brownies. He turned back to her. "That would be . . . ?" he prompted.

"Grace Slick of the Jefferson Airplane," Grace said. "And Harmony for—well, because my parents love music, and thought it was a cool middle name." She turned too, and winked at the girls.

"I think it's a pretty name," another girl added.

"Yes, it is," Brian said, still regarding Grace with an amused smile. Why did that smile make her feel like her insides were melting?

She had to get back to the tour and conclude with the girls before she went on the air. And not pay attention to the devastatingly masculine man who towered above her by a foot.

Smiling at the troop, she said, "Thank you so much for coming today. Tina has some gifts for you as you're leaving— WQNJ Frisbees for you girls, and coffee mugs for your moms." She met the glance of Paulette Nichols, one of the chaperones, whose daughter she had come to know well in the last six months.

"What do we say, girls?" Paulette asked.

A chorus of thank-yous reverberated in the corridor. As they slowly filed out, holding the Frisbees and coffee mugs, Grace gave quick hugs to LaShone, and Maritza, her roommate Yadira's "little sister". "Yadira and I will see you guys next week!" she told the two.

Charles and Brian called good-bye to the girls as they trooped out into the cold January afternoon.

Grace turned. Brian had moved so he stood right behind her.

She tilted her head to look up at him, inhaling the scent of a subtle but masculine cologne.

"You certainly have an unusual name," he remarked.

"Yes, well, I like it," she said lightly. Her heart was beating more rapidly than usual. "And it goes well with my special show, so I use it on the radio."

"Your special show?"

"The Love, Peace, and Happiness Hour. The show I do from five to six," Grace said. "That's when I play music from the late sixties and early seventies. From three to five, and then from six to seven, I play the regular oldies from the fifties through the eighties. But during my show, I concentrate on the music of those idealistic years."

She recognized the note of pride in her voice. The show had been her own idea, and Charles Armstrong had liked it. Apparently, so did their listeners. The response had been enthusiastic, and she now had a large audience for the show.

"You know," she finished. "That time when the ideals of peace, love, and happiness were so prominent."

"In other words, the hippie era." Brian said. Grace thought she detected a dry note in his voice.

"Well, yes," Grace said. "When everyone believed that love was all you need, as the Beatles said. And world peace and happiness were possible. There was a song with that title—I play it as the show starts—by the Chambers Brothers."

"Love, peace, and happiness." This time there was no denying the sardonic tone of Brian's voice. "Yes, I've heard your show."

Grace stared at him. "You sound so cynical." She said it quietly, trying to keep her voice from sounding as shocked as she felt. Who didn't believe in those ideals? Or at least yearn for them? He sounded . . . almost bitter, she thought.

Brian's handsome face had taken on a skeptical expression. "Yeah, well," he said, his tone dropping lower, "it's hard to believe in those ideals when life has taught you otherwise."

Grace's mouth dropped open. She shut it hastily. She'd met people who felt the same, of course. People who looked at the negatives rather than the bright side of things.

Somehow, it shocked her that Brian was one of those people.

And the disappointment that swept through her core at his words surprised her.

"Happiness, yes," Brian was continuing. "That's possible. World peace . . . highly unlikely."

"And love?" The question was out of her mouth before she could stop it.

"Love?" Brian's expression darkened. "Improbable. In fact, impossible. At least, for some people."

Poor guy. It was the first thought that flew into Grace's head. What had happened to him to make him so cynical about love?

And why did it bother her so much?

"I don't agree," she whispered. "Everyone is capable of finding love."

"Platitudes from the anti-war era." Brian's eyes met hers squarely, and she recognized the challenge there.

Beside her, Charles coughed.

She had momentarily forgotten his presence. Glancing at the friendly face of her employer, Grace collected herself. "I'd better get ready to go on the air," she said.

She tilted her chin up further, standing as straight as she'd learned in ballet classes. "Why don't you listen to my show? It might change your outlook," she suggested to Brian. Although her words were as challenging as his, she said them in a kind, soft tone. She didn't want to fight with the man. Only to convince him he was wrong.

"I always listen to the station." Brian's words were unadorned but firm.

"That's good." She left it at that. Smiling once more, she finished, "I'm glad to meet you. I'm sure I'll see you soon." She glanced at Charles, noting his expression looked highly amused. Had he found the interchange between her and Brian funny? she wondered. "Thanks for letting LaShone's troop visit today."

"I always like it when young people visit," Charles said. "It opens up the world of radio to them."

"And gets us some more listeners," Brian added.

"True." Charles said. "You don't have to be old to listen to oldies. It's some of the best music ever written."

"I agree." Grace smiled at them both. "See you later."

She left them in the hall and walked past the reception area to the studio. Since the speakers were always turned to their station, she could hear the song that was playing—a favorite by the Supremes. Quietly slipping into the small room, she greeted Will, the late-morning and early-afternoon DJ. He'd stayed later today so she could give the tour. He nodded back, and handed her the headphones.

"Here." He also gave her a slip of paper with news about an accident on Route 46 tying up afternoon traffic. "Just got this." His tone was low.

"Okay. I'll announce it right after the news," Grace said, sliding into her seat.

The song ended, and the radio station's call letters were announced, followed by the voice of Jan from the newsroom. Grace would have a few minutes of national and local news and weather before coming on the air.

She had already chosen music for today's show. But as she sat there, looking at the CDs she'd lined up, Grace had a new thought. She decided to add one song. It was a personal favorite, so she had no trouble finding it.

She listened to the news, but her mind raced all the while. She was still tingling from the encounter with Brian, and unsure why. She'd met plenty of handsome men before. She had even liked some of them.

Including Todd. Now *that* was a mistake.

But she'd never had quite so instantaneous a reaction to anyone she'd just met as she had to Brian.

She mulled over their meeting. It was sad, she thought, that Brian seemed so skeptical about life and love. Perhaps he'd just never met the right person. Or he'd been hurt in a previous relationship.

Growing up, Grace had never tired of listening to the story about her parents' meeting. Her mother loved to tell how she'd met Grace's father, how they'd been instantly attracted and fallen quickly in love. Grace had always wondered if someday the same thing would happen to her. It had happened to her brother Don, now happily engaged to his girlfriend.

She'd never expected to find herself attracted to someone who was so obviously not interested in romance.

She suppressed a groan. Well, she thought, perhaps he just needed to find the right person.

On that thought, the engineer in the next room signaled through the glass. She'd be on the air in half a minute.

She straightened slowly, anticipation curling within her. She might not be visible to the listeners, but she was on stage nonetheless. She loved this part of her job. She smiled, knowing it would show in her voice.

Carl, the engineer, signaled again, and the theme for her show began.

She waited for the song to play for a half minute. Then she leaned toward the microphone.

"Hello, and welcome to our Friday afternoon edition of the Love, Peace, and Happiness Hour!" she said brightly. "Your hour to relax and unwind after a hard day's work. It's Friday, and we anticipate the weekend!" She paused for only a split second. "This is our show where you're invited to tune into the music from the late sixties and early seventies, and recall those years when everyone believed in peace, love, and happiness, and strived to attain those ideals." The music slowly faded.

"This is your flower child, Grace Harmony, host of the show," Grace continued enthusiastically. "I have some great songs lined up for your listening pleasure. First, a traffic note: there are back-ups on Route 46 headed west from Netcong to Hackettstown, all due to a fender-bender at the bottom of the Hackettstown Mountain. Expect some delays; and as our weatherman Tom said, sleet should be arriving later so watch out for those slick spots!"

She went on. "For those of you new to the show, we showcase the music of that era that was so full of idealism. If you have a favorite, let us know! We'll see if we can squeeze it in near the end of the show. Any questions? I'm this station's resident flower child. My parents met at the Woodstock festival, and I grew up listening to this music. It's the best."

She grinned as she continued. "Now, those of you who've listened in before know I'm named for my mom's favorite female vocalist, Grace Slick of the Jefferson Airplane and Jefferson Starship. And of course I love their music! Now we're going to hear one of their most popular songs." She reached for the CD. "Oddly enough, I met someone recently who just might need what the song suggests: 'Somebody to Love'!" She inserted the CD in the "cart" machine and turned the dial as she finished speaking.

As Grace Slick's powerful voice vibrated through the air, Grace leaned back in her seat. She wondered if she looked as mischievous as she felt. It was always fun to spontaneously choose a song that fit the moment, and this one seemed to suit her meeting with Brian. He definitely needed somebody to love.

Brian marched into his office and shut the door. His heart was thumping harder than usual.

He knew it was because of his encounter with Miss Grace Harmony Norwood. And he wasn't pleased.

He threw the papers he was clutching on his desk. They landed in front of the single photo there, the one someone had taken last year of him with his sister, Lois. Sighing, he dropped down onto his seat.

What was it about this female disc jockey that had caused his heart to beat erratically? That had his whole body buzzing as if he'd had an electrical shock?

She had a beautiful face. He could admit that. Perfect features, big blue-gray eyes, and an appealing mouth that looked like it was constantly curving up in smiles. Her hair had been drawn back, but wisps of chocolate brown had escaped and framed her face enchantingly.

But she was just a kid! She must have been straight out of college. Brian knew she had to be at least twenty-two unless she'd graduated early, but she looked more like eighteen, with her petite stature, young face—and innocent idealism shining through her eyes.

He shifted in his chair. He'd met plenty of beautiful women. Heck, he'd dated his share of them. Usually they were sophisticated and amusing. He had fun and that was that. He didn't plan to get serious with any of them. He'd slipped once, with Victoria. But he wouldn't make that mistake again.

Grace might be beautiful, but she was much too young to interest him. Too young and idealistic, he told himself firmly, and leaned down to study the top paper with the lists of advertising prospects.

What he needed, he thought, was a new event to bring some life into the radio station. Not that it wasn't lively, and the ads were doing well enough. But he wanted to improve on that, make it more vital, even more important to the surrounding communities, bring further excitement to the listening audience. And generate some big time advertisers.

Fortunately, Charles Armstrong was in agreement.

It was a challenge, one he looked forward to meeting. His old job in New York had grown boring, the same-old same-old, dealing with all those hyper people who were on a treadmill of daily living. Taking a job out here, in northwest New Jersey, closer to his sister and the skiing he loved, had been a decision he'd pondered for a while. Finally, after the holidays, he'd cut lose from the old grind. Now here he was, and he was glad. From the moment he'd started at WQNJ he'd felt at home, and was enjoying his job even more than he'd expected.

The news ended, and he heard Grace on the radio. Her voice was warm and mellow. If he was one of their listeners, he'd feel like he was an old friend of Grace's, he thought. It was easy to picture her, dressed in her silly hippie outfit, smiling at her audience.

He heard her talk about the show. Resident flower child? he thought with amusement. Yes, that described her perfectly. It was no surprise to learn her parents had met at the Woodstock concert. No wonder she clung to the ideals of love, peace, and happiness.

Maybe if she was older—he quickly pushed the thought aside. No way. She was a kid. She might be pretty and lively, but she was way too young for him. He was twenty-nine, after all.

Grace was too young—and too idealistic. Life hadn't squashed her spirit yet.

And yet, something about her spirit sparked his curiosity.

He listened as Grace spoke.

". . . oddly enough, I met someone recently who just might need what the song suggests: 'Somebody to Love'!"

Somebody to love? Someone she met recently—could she possibly mean *him?*

Brian grimaced at the speakers in his office.

"What does she know about love?" he muttered darkly. "She's just a kid!"

". . . and we end today's Love, Peace, and Happiness Hour with this song, a request from Anne in Long Valley. Here's Norman Greenbaum with 'Spirit in the Sky'!" Grace announced.

The song began, and she leaned back. That was her special show for today. Following would be the long version of the news, then a syndicated radio columnist with his cheerful thoughts for the day. She'd have time to eat dinner before coming back to the mike.

She loved her job, and had been excited to find one close to her hometown. Her family usually listened to WQNJ, and when Grace had pretended to be a disc jockey when she was young, she always imagined working here. After college she'd been offered several jobs, but this was the one that appealed the most. She came home to Stanhope, started working, and after a few months, she and her very best friend Yadira had found a house to rent in nearby Landing.

The "Love, Peace, and Happiness" show had been her brainchild shortly after joining WQNJ, and it had steadily gained in popularity. With her career she had found not only success, but the peace and happiness she'd always strived for, just as the song said. As for love—well, she trusted she'd find it eventually. Despite her experience with Todd.

She'd find love with a little luck, she thought, standing up and stretching.

Why did Brian Talbot's face pop into her mind at that precise moment?

Grace frowned. He certainly wasn't a candidate for any future romance on her part. Why, the man had practically put down the idea of true love. Although he was the epitome of someone who needed somebody to love. If he had someone to love, he'd probably mellow out and be much happier.

As the song ended and she heard Jan's voice with the news, Grace slipped out of the studio and walked down the hall toward the staff room.

Charles was just leaving his office. "Grace!" he called, smiling as usual. "I was just going to see you. Come on into my office. I want to talk to you about something before I leave."

Grace followed her employer into his comfortable office, lined with photos of his wife, children, and grandchildren. Charles Armstrong, a robust man in his seventies, had settled in this area after World War Two. Coming from a wealthy New York family, he'd taken an inheritance and started the radio station many years ago, building it up gradually. Too energetic to retire, he now kept his hand in many aspects of running the station, though he delegated a lot of the more mundane work to his employees.

Grace slid into a leather chair as Charles leaned against the desk, which was overflowing with papers and folders.

"That was a brilliant idea!" he praised.

"What?" Grace asked, perplexed.

"The idea to find somebody for Brian Talbot! What a promotion!"

"Find somebody—"

"Yes," he continued. "We can find Brian a girlfriend!"

Chapter Two

Grace's mouth dropped open. Shutting it quickly, she stared at Charles, who was smiling widely. He leaned forward.

"I heard everything you and Brian were saying about Love, Peace, and Happiness," he said. "Then when you started your show and made that quip about meeting someone who needs somebody to love, I thought, this is it! What a great idea! Especially with Valentine's Day coming next month. We'll find a girlfriend for Brian!" His eyes sparkled with enthusiasm for the idea.

"You want to use the radio station to find somebody for Brian to love?" She knew her voice sounded as shocked as she felt. "I never meant—"

"Oh, I know you just meant it as a little inside joke," Charles said, waving away her protests as if they were stray snowflakes. "But I thought, we can turn this into a new promotion for the radio show. You know, find a Valentine for the newest member of our radio team!" He beamed at Grace.

Grace's heart felt like it was tumbling down the side of the nearby mountain.

Find a Valentine for Brian Talbot? Somebody for him to love?

"You can't just find love for Brian through the radio," she

protested. "I mean, the man has to find his own true love, in his own time."

"Oh, I know we may not find him the love of his life," Charles agreed. "But we can at least find a girlfriend for him, someone to date. Think about it! Listeners can send in photos and descriptions of themselves—or someone else they think Brian would like. We'll pay for him to take a few of them out. Everyone will be listening to see who Brian chooses— we can build up the suspense! And the advertisers can get involved. Local restaurants, gift shops with Valentine merchandise—we can really get some mileage out of this." He rubbed his hands together. "Brilliant, Grace. Brilliant!"

If it was so brilliant, why did she have this empty feeling in the pit of her stomach? Why didn't she feel as gleeful as Charles did? Grace rubbed her own hands together. They had turned cold.

She spoke cautiously. "I did say it as kind of a little joke. But I never meant to find a girlfriend for Brian. After all, I'm sure he's perfectly capable of finding his own. He's handsome, the kind of guy who attracts women . . ." Her voice wound down.

But Charles was in the throes of the idea. "I'm sure the listeners will be excited about this," he mused. "Finding a date for someone like him—it'll be no problem."

"I don't think he'll like the idea!" This time Grace spoke more forcefully. She was beginning to feel a strange, almost panicky sensation in her stomach. She wanted to jump up and pace around the room. She gripped the edges of the chair instead. "In fact, I think he'll hate it." She was sure of that. "And you can't follow through without his cooperation. Really," she finished, "just forget I ever said it."

"Forget it? Of course not," Charles said. "As far as him liking the idea—we'll call him in and see what he says. He's still here."

"I don't think—" she protested, but Charles was already striding to the door. Yanking it open, he walked down the hall, and she heard him rap on the door to Brian's office. "Brian, could you come into my office for a minute or two?"

In a moment Charles returned, continuing to look pleased. Grace pressed her hands together.

Uh-oh. What had she done? Brian would despise the idea, she was certain.

She steeled herself against what she was sure was going to be an unpleasant encounter.

She was hoping that seeing him for the second time would have no special effect on her. That the first flutterings she'd felt had been a fluke.

But when he walked into the office a minute later, her heart did a somersault.

Even with the puzzled expression on his face, he looked handsome. He had removed his tie and jacket and opened the top of his shirt. He looked more than handsome, she admitted to herself. Devastatingly masculine, strong and—

She stopped that train of thought. In a minute, she guessed, he was going to be very annoyed. Maybe very angry.

"Grace said something on her show which got me thinking," Charles began. Grace noticed he was no longer crediting her with the idea. An attempt to keep Brian from getting annoyed at her? she wondered. "And I came up with a brilliant idea which, I think, could lead to an interesting advertising campaign. Interesting and fun—for the listeners, and you."

Grace saw Brian's golden-hazel eyes flicker toward her, then back to Charles. "Go ahead. I'm listening."

"With Valentine's Day in a little over a month, we could make this an interesting seasonal promotion," Charles continued. "We can try to find you a girlfriend by Valentine's Day! Or at least, a date."

Silence.

Grace looked from Brian to Charles and back again.

Brian's mouth was set in a straight line. She waited to see if he would burst into anger. Or, like the station's previous advertising manager, start complaining.

Brian did neither.

"Well, what do you think?" asked Charles.

"I'm thinking." The words were clipped, reluctant. Grace suspected he was annoyed and holding it in. He glanced at her again. Did she imagine an accusing look in those eyes?

And why did men always get such lush dark lashes?

She bit her lip. Why on earth was she having these crazy thoughts? For heaven's sake, she had run into plenty of good-looking men before. She'd had several casual boyfriends over the years, although no one since she'd broken up with Todd.

But she'd never had quite this strong a reaction to someone she'd just met.

It was because Brian was older, she assured herself. Older and masculine and definitely more sophisticated then the guys she was used to dating.

"I don't like the idea." Brian's voice held a raspy note.

"From a personal or business standpoint?" Charles questioned.

"Personal." He looked pointedly at Grace.

"I didn't think you'd like the idea," she said, feeling her body relax against the chair. She brushed back a lock of hair that had come loose.

"And from a business standpoint?" Charles was continuing.

Brian shifted his position. "From a business standpoint, I'd like to hear more."

Grace sat straight up, quelling a gasp.

"We'd start the campaign almost immediately," Charles began, as if he'd been thinking of this plan for days. "Find a Valentine for the newest member of our radio team! Single women could send in photos and descriptions of themselves, their hobbies, etc. Or their friends can nominate them. You can go over these or—" Here he glanced at Grace. "—Grace can help weed through them and select the best candidates, according to your interests."

Grace made a sound of protest but Charles continued on.

"From those she picks, you chose a few—let's say three—women to date. The station will pay for you to take them to dinner—or perhaps we'll find some local restaurants to sponsor you—and then you'll choose one lucky woman to be your date for Valentine's Day. And maybe you'll even want to keep dating her!" Charles leaned against his desk. He wore a satisfied smile.

Grace slowly turned her head, meeting Brian's eyes.

"I don't think—" she began.

Brian's expression had darkened as he listened to Charles. He leaned against the wall, folding his arms.

"I have no trouble finding my own girlfriends," he said dryly. For just a moment, Grace thought she caught a flash of humor in his eyes. "As a matter of fact, I prefer to pick my own dates and not to get fixed up. However," he went on, "I have to admit that from a marketing perspective, it's an interesting idea."

Grace clenched her hands. He couldn't mean—

"Then you'll do it?" Charles asked eagerly.

"I'll think about it," Brian said. "And I'll let you know on Monday." He focused his glance on Grace. "Was this your idea, Flower Child?"

"No!" Grace declared. "I mean, I played that song as a little joke, but I never meant that I'd try to find you a girlfriend—"

"I'm surprised," he interrupted. "I thought that's what you'd *want* to do. Help everyone in the world find love, peace, and happiness."

Grace felt herself flushing. "Just because I believe in love doesn't mean I'm an expert at finding it." Her relationship with Todd was proof of that, she thought.

"But you do believe in true love." Once again the challenge wove forcefully through his voice.

"Yes, I do." She met his look squarely with her own. Again, she thought she saw a glimmer of laughter. At her? At her ideals? At this situation?

She wasn't sure.

"I don't." He shrugged elaborately. "But," he turned back to Charles, who appeared to be observing them with keen interest, "the idea lends itself to a lot of marketing possibilities. I'll think it over, and get back to you on Monday, as I said."

"Good." Charles's tone was firm. Grace had a sneaking suspicion that Charles thought he'd already won Brian's consent. "Let me know as soon as you can. We have to get things rolling immediately if we're going to do this."

"Of course." Brian turned back to Grace. "Are you ready to help if I agree?"

That caught her off guard. For a moment, Grace was unsure of what to say—an unusual situation for her.

"I—"

"Of course she is." Charles smiled at her fondly. "Grace is an intrinsic member of our team here."

Grace lifted her chin up, and met the challenge she saw gleaming in Brian's eyes.

"Yes, I'll help find you a Valentine," she said.

Grace sat at her desk in the office she shared with several of the other disc jockeys, studying the script for an advertisement she would record later in the afternoon. It was an amusing ad for a florist. She played the part of the wife who didn't like the gifts her husband had been getting her for Valentine's Day, and was dropping hints about getting flowers this year.

The ad was clever and funny. The note on top, from Charles, said she'd be doing the voiceover with Will, the morning DJ. Charles mentioned that Brian had written the ad.

Thoughts of Brian Talbot had floated through her mind a lot during the weekend. Even though she'd been busy—chores and shopping with her roommate and best friend, Yadira; the movies on Saturday night with her sister Crystal; and doing laundry and reading on Sunday—she'd thought about Brian more often than she liked.

She wondered for the hundredth time if he was going to go along with Charles Armstrong's zany plan.

She'd find out soon enough, she told herself, and focused her attention on the script in her hand.

When the rap sounded on her door, she almost jumped.

"Come in," she said, laying down the papers.

Brian Talbot entered the room, shutting the door behind him.

He looked as handsome as she recalled. Today he wore a forest-green sweater, a plaid green-and-beige shirt collar sticking up underneath, and beige slacks. His eyes, behind his glasses, looked more brown today.

"Hi," he said, smiling.

"Hi," she replied, wondering why her heart seemed to be leaping into her throat.

He hesitated, and she got the feeling he was appraising her.

"How are you?" she asked, keeping her voice smooth. She never felt this kind of turmoil around a guy. She certainly wasn't going to let him know.

"Fine. How are you, Flower Child?"

"Don't call me that." Grace felt oddly annoyed.

"Why not? You call yourself that. I heard Will and Charles refer to you that way when they were talking about the voice-over for the ad." He gave her an innocent look, stepping closer.

She caught a whiff of the subtle, masculine cologne or aftershave he was wearing. The same kind as last week. He must have a favorite brand, she thought irreverently. Then, brushing aside the thought, she concentrated on the here and now. "I am the station's resident flower child," she admitted. "I'm proud of it. I love the music from that era, and the hopes and dreams everyone shared to make a better world." She frowned as she caught the laughter in his face. "You're making fun of me," she accused.

"No," he said, shaking his head, "I'm not. I'm just teasing."

"Well, I don't like it."

He was silent, and she had a feeling that it wasn't the last time he was going to tease her.

"Do you want something?" she asked, her voice still tinged with annoyance.

"I wanted to tell you I spoke to Charles. I'm going to go along with his Valentine's date plan."

Brian watched Grace as he said the words. For a moment, her beautiful face got paler, and her blue-gray eyes widened. He could swear she was surprised and not pleased by the idea.

Seeing her sitting there at her desk had jolted all his senses just as much as meeting her on Friday had.

Thoughts of Grace had poked through his mind on and off all weekend. Even while skiing with his closest friend, Joe, he'd found himself daydreaming about Grace. And he couldn't imagine why on earth a kid like her had captured his attention.

Finally, he came to the conclusion that when he saw her again, he'd realize there was nothing special there to daydream about.

His theory had just flown out the window along with the airwaves from the radio station.

She looked even prettier than he remembered. She was small-boned, her delicate hands gripping some papers. Her facial features were utterly feminine, her big eyes a beautiful shade of gray-blue, her nose cute and pert and her mouth pink and kissable.

He steeled himself against that thought. Kissable? What had gotten him thinking this way?

She did look less like a kid today, he observed. Her thick hair, a chocolate-brown color, curved just above her shoulders, reminding him of some delectable fudge. Wearing her hair down did make her look a little older. Or maybe it was the oval gold hoop earrings peeking through her hair and the mysterious perfume that made her seem older.

She wore a bright orange sweater today, with fringe around the cuffs and collar. She still looked hip and offbeat.

"How old are you?" He hadn't meant to ask. The words simply leapt out of his mouth.

She looked startled. "Twenty-four. Why? How old are you?"

"Twenty-nine." Too old, he told himself. Too old.

"Why do you ask?" she persisted.

"Just curious. You look so young." He changed the subject. "We have to start work on this dating thing right away.

Charles wants to announce it tomorrow on the radio during your show."

Something flashed across her face, and was gone.

"All right. Where do we begin?"

"With a list of what I would like in a woman I date," Brian said.

"Why don't you pull up a chair?" Her voice was exceedingly polite. What was she thinking? he wondered.

He sat down, and she pushed aside some papers that were piled on her desk.

He spotted a large framed photo of Grace with three other young people.

"Friends of yours?" he asked.

She glanced at the picture, and a smile lit her face. "My sister and two brothers."

"Your sister looks a lot like you," he said, sitting down. "Are you twins?"

"No, Crystal's the oldest, then Don, then me. Paul's the baby."

"Well, you look a lot alike." He studied the photo for a moment. The other young woman was the same height as Grace and had almost identical features, but her hair was a much lighter color and it looked like her eyes were hazel, not blue. "Was she named for someone famous too?"

"Crystal? Her name's Crystal Blue." Grace rose gracefully, and began rummaging through a stack of papers and folders. As she did, the sweater molded against her, and he realized she had a beautiful figure. She leaned forward, producing a long, legal-sized pad of yellow paper, then opened a drawer and grabbed a pen. Her perfume drifted toward him.

"Crystal Blue?"

"Crystal Blue Norwood." She looked back up at Brian, and grinned suddenly. "Crystal Blue. As in Crystal Blue Persuasion."

"Crystal Blue Persuasion?" he repeated, wondering if he sounded like an idiot.

"The song. By Tommy James and the Shondells." Now her

smiled widened. "My parents liked the song. It's about love, and peace . . ."

"Of course." Vaguely, he remembered the song. He'd heard it played at least once since he'd started work at WQNJ. "Crystal Blue, and Grace Harmony . . . your parents definitely chose unusual names for their children."

"Yes, for all of us." Grace tossed her hair, grinning up at him. "Don is Donovan Peace Norwood. Donovan for the singer. And Paul's full name is Paul Brotherhood Norwood. Paul for Paul McCartney, and Paul Butterfield."

Peace and Brotherhood? Oh boy. Grace's parents must have been real hippies!

Brian whistled. "Wow. You come from an interesting family background."

"Yes. How about you?"

"Me?" He didn't really want to talk about his family. "Oh, the usual. Two parents, my sister Lois, and me. A traditional, upper-middle class family."

"Where'd you grow up?" she asked.

"In Bergen County."

"Where?"

He named the town. He was startled to see Grace's head come up suddenly. She stared at him, and her look darkened. What difference did it make where he came from? he wondered.

She bent her head again. "Well, what are your hobbies?" she asked.

"Skiing," he answered promptly.

"You can do plenty of that in this part of New Jersey."

"I know. That's one of the reasons I moved out here."

"Really?" she asked, scribbling on the pad of paper.

"Yes. I spend so much time skiing out here in winters and boating during the summers that I decided I might as well live out here."

"And that's why you looked for a job here?" she continued.

"That, and the fact that I was tired of the rat race of the

city. And I thought I'd like to live closer to my sister. And my friend Joe."

Grace regarded him. Her face was beautiful, and a youthful curiosity shone from her eyes.

"Where do they live? And what about your parents?"

"Lois lives in Newton. Joe lives in Panther Valley, and found me a condo there to rent until I buy one. My father died a few years ago, and my mother lives in Florida during the winter." Brian shifted again. "But you don't need to know about them."

Pink tinged her cheeks. She looked adorable, he thought.

"No, I guess not. I was just wondering. Okay . . . you said you like sailing too?" She returned to making notes.

"Yes. And this part of the state offers both."

"True." Her head was bent, and he couldn't see her expression. Then she looked up at him, and again he felt something skitter up his spine. Something, a feeling of . . . what? He couldn't define it. He only knew he was feeling *something*.

"Where'd you go to college?" Her eyes were fastened on him.

"NYU. And I got my MBA there too."

"What kinds of books do you like to read?"

"Mysteries, and suspense."

She scribbled. "Your favorite music is . . ."

"This station's, of course." He grinned, and she glanced up again and met his eyes. She smiled back, and for a moment the air between them hummed. It was as if sound waves melodically bounced between them, playing a silent but harmonious piece of music.

He broke into the moment. "I enjoy rock and roll, both classical and newer types. I guess you could say I like everything from the Beatles and Stones and Doors to today's artists like Smash Mouth."

"They have that traditional rock sound," Grace agreed, writing quickly. "Any other types of music?"

"Oh . . . Broadway tunes, I guess, and some classical," he said. He leaned back in his chair, watching her feminine hand move as she wrote. The only jewelry she wore, he noticed, besides her gold hoop earrings was a simple gold ring with a red stone. Her birthstone, he guessed.

"So, when you're not skiing, or sailing, or reading or listening to music, what else do you like to do?" she asked.

"Tease beautiful women like you."

Her head shot up, and she stared at him.

Tease beautiful women like *her?*

Grace felt her heart bounce. Brian Talbot had called her beautiful!

"You think I'm beautiful? Oh—you're teasing me again." She tried to make her voice sound lighthearted, but was afraid she hadn't succeeded.

She shouldn't be so pleased by the compliment. She'd been called beautiful before, but coming from Brian, the words held more meaning.

"You are, you know. Beautiful." He studied her, his expression growing serious. "But you must have had dozens of guys tell you that."

"Some did," she admitted.

"I bet it was more than just some."

"Well, yes, but a lot of them were only interested in my looks." She changed positions. "We're not here to talk about me, though." Her pulse was jumping as much as her heartbeat. She tried to calm the fluttering within her. "What are you looking for in a woman?"

He seemed startled. "What do you mean?"

"In a woman you want to date?"

"Oh . . ." He hesitated, pondering the thought. "I'd like to go out with someone who shares some of my interests. She should be friendly, and warm, and have a good sense of humor. And be attractive."

Grace bent her head, continuing her notetaking. "Anything you don't like?"

"I don't like women who are more interested in money and status than in people."

The way he said the words, with a peculiar intensity, made

Grace raise her head to stare at him. His hazel eyes sparked behind his glasses, and his mouth had taken on an almost grim look. His male scent reached her again.

"I don't like people like that either," she agreed quietly, wondering if she had touched on a sore spot.

He seemed to realize he was sounding emotional, because his expression became less guarded, and Grace guessed he was trying to appear indifferent. "There's too many self-centered people in the world."

"That's true." She made her tone soothing. "So what are you looking for in a future spouse?"

He stared at her. "Spouse? I'm really not interested in marriage." His tone was flat. "We're trying to find me a date here, not a wife." A biting note crept into his voice as he finished.

Grace knew immediately that she had hit a sensitive spot. He obviously didn't like the topic of marriage. Why?

"You're right," she agreed smoothly. "We're concentrating on a date. I was just wondering why a handsome man like you hadn't gotten married already. Or were you married before?"

"No. I have no desire to get married," he said tersely.

That was a topic that needed exploring, Grace thought— though probably at a later date. She tucked that thought away in her mind for future pondering.

Mentally sighing, Grace took another tack. "Are there any other sports you enjoy?"

"I play golf sometimes, though it's way behind skiing and boating." His posture relaxed a tiny bit. "And I enjoy swimming."

Grace continued to ask him what she felt were nonthreatening questions. She learned Brian enjoyed watching football and basketball and hockey, and his favorite TV shows were those about police and lawyers. And he liked the old comedy classics from the golden age of TV. He had traveled to England, France, and Italy several times and hoped to visit Hawaii next.

"Well, this should be plenty of info," she said a few minutes later. "We can write up a short bio on you, and get it on the air by Wednesday—maybe even tomorrow."

"And I can start finding advertisers interested in the concept," Brian said. He stood up. "You'll let me see what you write before you air it, won't you?"

"Sure," Grace agreed. Standing, Brian towered over her. She felt tiny and almost inconsequential. She didn't care for the feeling.

He's probably used to sophisticated women. The thought sprang from the back of her brain.

"Do you like sophisticated women?" she asked, rising from her seat and tilting her chin up.

For a moment, Brian looked almost amused. "Sophisticated women? Exactly what do you mean?"

Grace knew exactly what she meant. The type of women who'd been around, she thought. The kind who had been everywhere and done everything.

But she didn't say it. Instead, she suggested, "Oh, you know the type—beautiful, cosmopolitan women. You know, the gutsy type from the city."

"I'm tired of the city," he replied, leaning against her desk. "As for beautiful and gutsy women . . . it seems the country has its share of those." His eyes sparkled as they regarded her.

Grace felt her cheeks flushing. He was teasing her again.

"I didn't mean—"

"You are beautiful . . . and I suspect you're gutsier than you appear," he continued. Leaning across the desk, he captured her chin in his hand, and turned her face up so their gazes locked.

An electrical current hummed through Grace, beginning where he touched her and fanning out through her face, her head, and down her body. The tingling raced along her limbs.

He brought his face closer. "You're sweet, Flower Child, and way too idealistic, but I think you're spirited too."

"I—" Grace couldn't think of a word to say. The moment hung suspended in the air, and she was conscious only of the thrumming throughout her being, of Brian's fingers touching her skin.

Then he pulled back, dropping his hand, and Grace was left with a sudden chill.

"Stop teasing me." The words came out defiantly. Why did this man have such a profound effect on her?

"I wasn't teasing." Brian's expression was serious. "I was admiring your youthful spirit. Too bad it has to change."

"What do you mean? My spirit doesn't have to change."

"Life will change it." The words came out clipped, and Grace glimpsed emotion in Brian's eyes. He looked ... disheartened, she decided.

"I don't agree." She whispered the words. "Life doesn't have to change a person's spirit."

"It usually does." His tone now held a note of weariness, and Grace's heart went out to Brian. Something, someone had changed his spirit, she was certain of it. Somewhere along the line, something had happened to crush this man's hopes.

"It doesn't have to.' Grace stepped around the desk, and moved toward Brian. Looking up at him, she met the disbelief in his face. "Many of us still have hopes and dreams, even though we've lived through disappointments." Her thoughts flitted to Todd.

Brian stepped back, putting space between them. "After you've had more disappointments, you won't feel the same." The bleak note in his voice touched a chord in her, and she had a crazy impulse to reach out and stroke his face reassuringly.

She forced her hand to remain at her side. His eyes looked wary.

"I don't agree with you," she repeated.

Brian grimaced, but said nothing. Taking another step backward, he said, "Let me see what you write up, okay?"

"Okay."

He turned and strode out of the room.

Grace returned to her desk, sinking into her chair. Her heart felt heavy, like it was weighted down by a burden, despite its rapid beating. And her arms felt shaky, as if Brian had set off an electrical charge that had totally zapped her.

Brian . . . what had happened to make him so cynical? she wondered.

And why did she care so much?

She knew why. It was because she was attracted to him. Despite his cynicism, she found him appealing and intriguing and she wanted to get to know him better. A whole lot better.

Which would be a mistake, she knew.

Because Brian came from the town next to the one where Todd grew up. And she knew exactly what kind of wealthy, privileged environment Brian had grown up in. The same kind of background that produced Todd.

Todd Elliot Carlisle . . . even thinking about him brought a bad taste to her mouth.

She had met Todd three years ago, the summer after her junior year of college. She was working at a big electronics store that summer, enjoying the discounts she got for music and videos. Todd had come in because he worked for the company. Or so Grace thought.

It turned out Todd's father was one of the owners of this chain of stores, and was grooming Todd to someday take his place. So Todd was learning different aspects of the business. Todd had pursued her, and they began dating.

At first, Grace was flattered by Todd's attention. The flowers, the dinners at fancy restaurants—she couldn't help feeling flattered by it all. She pushed aside some nagging doubts about the way he seemed to go overboard, even when he bought her an expensive necklace.

He admitted, in his boyish but charming way, that he'd been attracted to Grace because she was "different" from the girls he'd known. "You are unique," he'd told her more than once. "You really go your own way."

Grace gradually noticed, however, that Todd treated a lot of people with disdain. After hearing him make negative remarks about people from different ethnic groups, she introduced him to her best friend. When Todd later made a disparaging remark about Hispanic people, Grace confronted him.

To her horror, she learned that Todd was even more prejudiced than she'd suspected. He felt superior to people from every ethnic group but his own. Listening to the nasty put-downs he made, Grace had no trouble making up her mind. She could *never* have a relationship with someone so closed-minded, so prejudiced.

She broke up with Todd that night.

Now, she wondered, was Brian another Todd? Had his similar background left him with the same discriminations?

She decided to make it a point to find out. Before she got any more ideas about Brian.

It was clear that Brian Talbot thought she was an innocent youngster who was naive to the ways of the world. And he had no interest in getting to know her better. He made that very obvious.

Which might be the best thing for both of them.

Grace slouched in her chair. His opinion bothered her. In that instant she knew she'd like to be one of the women Brian would go out with. In order to get to know him, she told herself hastily, and to have a fun time.

But there seemed little chance of that. Although Brian probably wouldn't limit himself to dating only sophisticated women, he certainly didn't want to go out with someone he regarded as a kid, full of youthful idealism. Grace was sure of that.

Which left her out in the cold.

She sighed. *Oh well,* she thought. They might have had a good time together, but if he was anything like Todd, she didn't want to go out with him. She definitely didn't want to get tangled up with someone like that again.

She would just have to find someone else for him to date. Maybe someone who could chase away that bleak look from his eyes, eliminate that pessimistic attitude.

Who would neatly fit that role?

Grace sighed again.

* * *

Brian stalked back into his office, shut the door, and sat down in his chair.

What on earth was wrong with him?

Grace Norwood was turning his world upside-down.

He couldn't understand it. He'd met plenty of good-looking women before. Plenty of beautiful, bright women. Even some who were optimistic.

But he'd never met anyone who caused the kind of reaction in him that Grace did. A feeling of sailing through the air. Of total awareness, of being alive. A feeling that, if he tried, he could shake off his old, preconceived notions.

He had almost kissed her. Touching her soft skin, her face turned up to his, he had come this close to bending down and capturing her mouth.

The whole thing was making him dizzy. She had that strong an effect on him. Like she was tilting his entire self, his soul, his whole world.

Brian shook his head. He had to snap out of this. Whatever it was, whatever magical spell seemed to spin around them when he was near Grace, he had to fight it. He'd only get disappointed in the process, and Grace—Grace could get hurt too.

He leaned his head into his hands. He tried thinking about the clients he would see later and the phone calls he had to make.

But all he could think of was a kissable, rosy mouth; a pair of large, beautiful, blue-gray eyes; a pert nose; a musical voice . . .

Stop it, he told himself firmly. *Get your mind off of Grace.*

But she lingered in his mind long after he went back to his work.

Brian returned to the office late in the afternoon, after meetings with a restaurant owner and the owner of a new pet grooming parlor. The day was already darkening and the wind had picked up, making the day feel even chillier than it already was.

But the station was warm and humming with activity even at this late hour. As he entered the lobby, he could hear Grace on the radio, and stopped. Her voice was smooth and lilting, and he had to admit that she came across as an old friend on the airwaves. The listeners probably felt like they had known her for years.

He moved toward the studio, to see her through the glass, talking into the microphone.

". . . and here's one by Tommy Roe," she was saying. " 'Dizzy'. All about that wonderful, sudden rush of falling in love, when you feel off-balance and you don't even care!"

The song began playing, and he saw Grace turn her head in the booth. Their eyes met.

She smiled.

Darn if he didn't find himself smiling back. That the-world-is-a-groovy-place attitude of Grace's must be contagious.

He went back to his office and worked for a while on the two ads. Finally, stretching, he heard Grace's "Love, Peace, and Happiness" show come to an end, and the news began.

He still had work to do, but decided to put it aside for a while and have a bite to eat before finishing. He had half a sandwich left over from an early lunch that day, so he wandered back to the staff room.

He found Will there, munching on a slice of pizza. "Want some? I ordered a whole pizza but I can't finish it all now."

Will McPhearson, the early-afternoon DJ, was a hefty guy with long, shaggy blond hair and a sunny smile. He was probably about the same age as him, Brian guessed. Will had worked at the station for several years.

The smell of tomato sauce and tempting spices rose up to greet him from the pizza box. "I think I will," he said, grabbing a slice. "How much do I owe you?"

"You can pay next time," Will said, waving his hand.

Brian pulled up a chair at the large wooden table. "This is good," he said, chewing.

The door opened again, and Grace walked into the room.

No, not walked—floated, Brian observed. She walked with an ease and grace that matched her name exactly.

Will offered her pizza, and she accepted, taking bottled water out of the refrigerator. Sitting in between Will and Brian, she asked Brian how the ad campaign was going.

"I already have two restaurants and three florists committed to advertisements for this find-a-date promotion," Brian said. "And I'm contacting more businesses in the next few days."

"Okay." Grace smiled. "I have the announcement written up. I left a copy on your desk, and Charles is reading one now. We'll find you a special woman."

"Hey, what about me?" Will asked. "I haven't had a regular girlfriend since I broke up with Denise last year. I'm ready to find someone."

"Maybe we'll work on you next," Grace suggested with a chuckle.

"Spare him," Brian said.

Will laughed, as if he was enjoying the interchange between Brian and Grace. "Hey, when's your mother baking again?" he asked. Turning to Brian, he said, "Grace's mother makes the best brownies I've ever tasted."

"A real earth mother, huh?" Brian asked.

"You got that right," Will said. "Grace's mother is the best cook in the world. She sends in food occasionally. I wish my mom liked to cook."

"I'll probably see her later this week," Grace said. "By the way, my parents are having their annual Superbowl party in a few weeks, and she said to invite anyone from WQNJ who wanted to come."

"A chance to watch football and eat your mom's cooking? I wouldn't miss it," Will announced, taking another slice of pizza.

"You come too, Brian," Grace urged.

Brian was startled. At his last job, no one in the office socialized except for an occasional after-work drink. All the ad reps at the metro radio station had been extremely competitive, and chose to go their own way, sometimes clashing over territories and new business. There was just too much competition to make for a friendly atmosphere. And they'd had little to do with the DJs.

This was a lot nicer, he had to admit. He already liked the down-home feel of WQNJ much better. And the other two sales reps under him were more laid back, and stuck to their own accounts.

It might be fun to actually sit down in a different setting and get to know his coworkers.

"All right," Brian agreed. "Can I bring anything?"

"My mom said anyone who wants can bring sodas or snack food," Grace said. "They'll have a huge hero sandwich and my mom will make some side dishes."

"I'll bring soda," Will volunteered. "I can't cook," he told Brian.

"You never practice, that's why," Grace chided him lightly. "It's not so hard." She looked at Brian. "My parents live in Stanhope, not too far from here."

"I'm looking forward to meeting them already," Brian said. "Flower Parents of the Flower Children." But he said it in a good-natured voice.

"You should be so lucky to have parents like them!" Grace shot back. Her voice radiated pride.

"You're probably right," Brian replied lightly. He was curious about the people who'd raised such an idealistic daughter. They sounded very different from his own parents.

"What were your parents like?" Grace asked, curious. "I know your father died, but what was he like?"

"I didn't see him much. He was a corporate vice-president and constantly traveled," Brian said. He didn't want to discuss families. "My mother did a lot of volunteer work for a woman's league and the local hospital. What about you?" He switched the topic to Will's family.

"Oh, the usual. I grew up in Clark. My mom's a bit of a nervous person, and so are my two older sisters. My dad and

I are more relaxed." Will took a swig of his soda. "My dad's a gym teacher and baseball coach. My mom works in a bank."

Will set down his soda. "Hey, Grace, if you have a lot of women applying for the job of Brian's date, why not throw a few names my way?" His expression was almost wistful. "I'm serious."

"You're looking for a date?" Brian asked.

"Or maybe a lifetime partner. I'd like to settle down," Will admitted.

Grace regarded him. "I'll see what I can do," she said.

"We should have done this promotion for *you*," Brian said.

"But you're new to the station—a new, exciting persona," Will said. "We'll get more publicity using you!"

That was true, Grace thought, regarding the two men. Brian, being the exciting new-man-in-town, would naturally garner more attention than Will, who had worked here for at least three years. Not to mention that Brian was handsome and exceptionally masculine.

Not that Will was bad-looking. He simply didn't compare to Brian. He seemed more like everyone's big brother. While a woman could easily fantasize about being held in Brian's strong arms—

Quickly, Grace wiped that image from her mind. What was she, insane? Brian had made it clear he had little interest in long term relationships. And no interest in her.

But perhaps she could find someone for him, someone who could make his eyes light up and bring a smile to his serious face, even if it was just a temporary relationship, not true love.

She pondered the problem silently while the two men began talking about the teams slated for this year's football playoffs. Of course, there would probably be loads of women wishing to date Brian. But maybe she could find someone perfect for him, someone who really would make him think more positively.

He wouldn't want anyone overly sentimental, she decided. Someone who was positive, yet practical. Someone who would want to date but not get too involved, like Brian.

And then she thought of her sister.

Ah-ha! She almost said the words out loud.

Crystal had fallen for a guy over a year ago who turned out to be a real jerk. He conveniently forgot to tell people that he was married. When Crystal found out, she'd broken up with him. But she'd been hurt. She hadn't dated for a while.

Now she was starting to date, but only casually.

Brian might be good for Crystal. And Crystal might be just what Brian needed.

Grace wondered why she didn't feel more enthusiasm for the idea.

Chapter Three

Grace stared at the heap of papers on her desk. Since the announcement of the "Find a Valentine for Brian" promotion a week ago, a steady stream of letters and e-mails had arrived at the station. Tina had deposited these papers on Grace's desk for her to begin sorting.

Her heart slowly sank every time the mailman arrived with his stack of letters, and every time Charles handed her a fistful of printed e-mails from eligible women.

Grace reminded herself that this disheartened feeling was because it would be harder for her to get Brian to meet her sister. A lot of women were competing for a chance to date Brian. And that was the only possible reason she felt discouraged.

Was it her appealing description of him that made women want to date the new advertising director? Was it the photo of Brian that had appeared in the local newspaper and was posted on the WQNJ website?

Or was it just that there was an overabundance of eager females in the area?

She had a feeling it was all of the above. Plus, when Brian had spoken Thursday during Will's show, his deep voice had garnered the listeners' attention and a slew of new e-mails and letters had hit the station with the force of a loud rock band performance.

Grace sighed. It was her job, according to Charles, to look through those letters and select the ones she thought were most promising. Then she was to pass them to Brian, who would decide which lucky three women he'd meet for dinner. After those dates he would select one particular woman for his Valentine's date.

A number of restaurants were sponsoring the contest, providing free dinners. And for the grand finale, the Valentine's date, Brian and his chosen date would be picked up by an area limousine service, whisked away to dinner at an exclusive restaurant, then taken to a performance at a small, local theater. A tuxedo rental business was providing a tux for Brian to wear. All this for free, since the limo service, restaurant, theater, and tuxedo store would be featured in the announcements. The whole idea had taken on a life of its own.

Grace had put off sorting through the letters. But as she regarded the pile now threatening to engulf her desk, she knew she could put it off no longer. She sighed, and grabbed a handful of papers from the bottom of the stack.

An hour later, Grace leaned back and rubbed her head. She must have looked through a hundred papers, and only come up with five possibilities. She'd waded through an alarming number of women who were totally inappropriate—some as young as fifteen and a few in their sixties! Then there were the ones whose tone made her skeptical: they were looking for adventure; they wanted a new husband to help raise their children from a former marriage; two aspiring actresses who wanted the publicity; and in one case, a woman who boldly admitted she was looking for a fling to offset a boring marriage!

Many women had included photos of themselves, though it had been optional. Charles had told Grace to eliminate those women who were dressed in bikinis or who posed suggestively. He had also told Grace he'd torn up several letters that had arrived with nude photos!

"What is it with some people?" Charles had asked, shaking his head in disbelief.

Grace reminded herself to bring in a photo of her sister tomorrow. She'd already written a biography of Crystal, and hoped that Brian would chose her as one of his dates. He was going to chose three women by the end of the next week.

She took one last look at the five women she'd chosen from this first batch. She'd tried to pick not only the sophisticated-sounding women she was sure Brian would prefer; but some sincere-sounding types that she felt personally would be good for Brian.

There was Tara, a twenty-nine-year-old public relations manager for a nearby theme adventure park. Her photo revealed a woman with curly, long blond hair and a sophisticated appearance. Then there was Joanna, a sultry brunette aged thirty-four who taught aerobics and exercise programs.

Balancing these sophisticated types was Joyce, a thirty-year-old teacher in a nearby town who also enjoyed skiing; Ellen, a thirty-two-year-old young widow who owned her own pet-sitting business; and Monica, a thirty-year-old, attractive red-haired office manager for a legal firm in town.

Grace pushed aside the pile she had labeled as the rejects and neatly stacked the five promising entries for the station's contest.

As she gazed at the photos of the women, each with her own interests and talents, each ranging from attractive to downright beautiful, Grace wondered what had happened that these women, with the exception of the young widow, had been unable to find love on their own.

And a doubt began to wriggle in the recesses of her mind.

Would *she* ever find love?

Grace sat back.

"You can't hurry love," her mother used to tell her. "It comes at its own time." But then Grace would ask her mother to repeat the story about how she, Antonia Alberta, had met Matthew Norwood at the Woodstock concert in 1969. And before the festival was over, they'd known they had met their true loves.

Grace had always enjoyed hearing about her parents' meeting, their sudden romance, their defying of two sets of disapproving parents who had their own expectations, and their marriage outdoors in a small park surrounded by friends a year later.

And she'd always, always been sure that she, too, would meet the man of her dreams.

They would fall madly in love, marry, and live happily ever after. Like her parents, Toni and Matt Norwood.

Of course, she'd known her parents had had their ups and downs. Toni had worked as an inner-city kindergarten teacher, going to grad school part time while Matt finished law school. Both Toni's old-fashioned Italian family and Matt's wealthy, conservative family had broken off relations with the couple after their marriage. They'd struggled at first, then had their children, with Toni staying home and later substituting in day-care centers and elementary schools. And they'd remained happy, with a deep, abiding love for each other that people recognized and respected, even if their families never had. Today Grace's father was a well-known attorney and her mother taught several courses in early childhood education, and educating deprived children, at a local college.

Grace stared at the small photo of her parents. It stood on the desk beside the pictures of her siblings, and the photo of her golden retriever, Lincoln. Even after more than thirty years of marriage, the photo was evidence that Toni and Matt were still happy.

And that's what she wanted for herself.

The only question was, when?

She had had lots of dates and a number of boyfriends. And there was the unfortunate episode with Todd. But no one had made her heart truly sing.

Brian's face burst into her mind, and Grace let out a small groan.

Well, almost no one.

When would she find love?

Her brother Don had. Last year, he'd met Renee, and they had fallen in love. They were planning a wedding this summer.

Crystal was just starting to date again after her own bad experience, and Paul, who had just turned twenty, was probably too young.

And she . . . she hadn't met the love of her life yet.

Once again, Brian's face flashed across her mind.

She sighed. Against the background of a Beatles ballad, her sigh was unusually loud in the small room.

A knock sounded on the door.

Grace looked up, startled. She wasn't expecting anyone.

"Grace? Are you there?" Brian's deep voice, smooth and confident, could have been on radio, she thought. No wonder his voice had brought in so many responses.

She answered, "C'mon in."

Brian entered the room. Today he wore a navy sports jacket, blue shirt, and blue-and-yellow tie. As usual, Grace was struck by not only his good looks, but by the masculine aura that was so much a part of him. It wasn't just his broad shoulders, or confident stance. This was some indefinable quality that was intrinsic to Brian Talbot.

"Are you busy?" he asked, glancing at the papers spread on her desk.

"Not now. I just finished sifting through this first batch of prospective dates for you." Grace heard the note of discouragement in her voice.

Brian must have mistaken it for something else. "Tired?" he asked.

Grace shrugged. "Not really. I was just . . ." She stopped. The last person she should be confiding in was Brian, who obviously didn't believe in love.

"You were just . . . ?" he asked.

"Nothing." Another sigh escaped her lips before she realized it.

Brian stepped forward, and the cool, subtle scent of his

aftershave teased her again. "What?" His voice was quiet, yet sympathetic.

Grace focused on the photo of her parents. Brian moved to stand beside her chair, and laid a hand lightly on her shoulder. "You were just . . . ?" he repeated, his hand reassuring.

"Just wondering . . ." She shook her head. Where his hand rested, she felt warmth and compassion, and it seemed to penetrate her skin and flow through her veins.

"Are these your parents?" he asked, following her gaze.

"Yes."

"Ah . . . the earth mother and father," he said. As she straightened her spine, he quickly added, "I'm only teasing. They look like really nice people."

"They are the best." Grace turned and looked up at Brian. "They're still in love after more than thirty years of marriage and four kids."

"I see. Well, that's unusual, but lucky for them."

"Luck and some hard work," Grace said, studying Brian. "You don't believe in love, do you?"

"No, I don't." He stepped back, his hand dropping to his side.

"Why?" she asked, deliberately keeping her voice low and nonthreatening.

It was on the tip of Brian's tongue to say "because it doesn't exist," but he hesitated, as he saw the searching look in Grace's eyes. *She's just a kid,* he told himself again. *She obviously grew up in a happy household. She doesn't realize how rare that is.*

Today Grace was dressed in a long-sleeved, white T-shirt topped by a red crocheted vest. With her hair pulled back in red clips, she looked about sixteen.

Even so, since he'd entered the room, Brian had had the desire to touch her, to establish some physical connection to this young woman. It must be her warmth that drew him to her.

"Because . . . I've seen firsthand that love doesn't usually last." He allowed himself to say that much.

Grace regarded him seriously. "Oh."

He had no idea why, but that one-syllable word, said softly and with compassion, seemed to trip a switch in his soul.

"I grew up with parents who didn't get along." As Grace nodded, he felt the urge to continue. "I told you how my father was a corporate type. He traveled extensively and was rarely home. But when he was, he and my mother fought constantly. It wasn't pleasant."

"That must have been very tough for you." Her voice, melodious and caring, poured over him like sweet syrup over pancakes.

"Yes. Lois—my sister—and I had each other, so that helped, but home was not a comfortable place to be."

"I understand," Grace said quietly. "Yadira—my best friend—and I have another friend, Jenny, whose parents fought a lot. When we were in tenth grade, her parents split up, and the fighting only escalated. Poor Jenny was caught in the middle. I realize that homes like the one I grew up in are not the norm."

Brian nodded. "And then—" He halted. Somehow, the story of his parents' marriage had spilled out. And oddly, he didn't mind. At least, he didn't mind sharing it with Grace.

Grace was continuing. "Haven't you ever met anyone who made you feel differently, that there was hope?"

"Once." The angry word was out before he could stop.

Grace's eyes widened. "What happened?" Her voice was a whisper.

Brian sat on her desk, in the one corner that was free of paper clutter. "It didn't work out. I don't want to discuss it."

To his surprise, he saw a sheen of moisture in Grace's eyes. She reached out and touched his hand. "I'm sorry," she said gravely.

Her touch was light, her hand warm and reassuring. Brian realized with surprise that here was a young woman who really cared about others. Grace was a unique person in more ways than one. He had met very few sympathetic people at his previous job, and it felt surprisingly good to unburden and share his experience.

Their eyes met. The warmth there made him eager to know her even better.

He stretched his hand out and covered her hand. It felt surprisingly good tucked in his, and he leaned forward. A slightly fruity, innocent fragrance met him. She was wearing some kind of sweet, fruity cologne.

"Tell me why you were sighing," he said, keeping his own voice subdued.

Grace's expression looked surprised. "You really want to know?"

"Yes, I do." Her hand was incredibly soft. He clenched it.

"I . . ." Her voice drifted off. He waited.

"I . . . was just wondering," she began. She glanced over at the tallest stack of papers. "With all these eligible women out there, I was just wondering how long it would take *me* to find my true love."

Brian stared at her. It had never occurred to him that Grace would have trouble finding a boyfriend. "But you must have tons of guys pursuing you," he said. "You're beautiful and sweet—"

She shrugged. "Oh, I've had some, but not the Right One. It never bothered me before—I always trusted that I'd find him someday. Seeing this—" She tilted her head toward the piles of paper. "—I can't help wondering if I'll ever find someone for me." She glanced back up at him.

In that moment, Brian had an overwhelming urge to lean forward and kiss Grace.

He steeled himself, fighting the desire for more physical contact. To capture her rosy lips with his—

No. he told himself, squashing the impulse with effort. *I am not going to take advantage of this young girl when she's feeling down.*

He stood up abruptly, breaking the physical contact between them before he did anything rash. It required an enormous effort to let go of her.

"You will find someone," he said, as Grace regarded him with confusion. She was so young, so easy to read. "If you believe it, it will happen."

"You believe in positive thinking?" Grace asked, her voice still hushed.

"Yes," Brian said. "I believe you can do what you want in life—although love is probably the exception. But you'll have *plenty* of guys after you, and I have no doubt you'll find the right man. *And* he'll be damned lucky." The last words sprang out of his mouth as if by their own volition.

Now why on earth had he said that?

Grace's smile burst on her lips like the sun suddenly shining through the heavy winter clouds.

"Thank you." The words were simple, but her voice rang with sincerity.

"You're welcome." Despite the somber mood he'd felt when they touched on the subject of his family, Brian felt uplifted when he saw Grace smile. Her smile was sunshine, warming him.

For a moment they were silent, and again Brian fought the impulse to lean over and kiss Grace. He deliberately looked away, glancing at his watch for an excuse.

"I'd better get moving," he said. "I have a couple of appointments with advertisers."

"Good luck." Again, her voice rang out warmly.

"Thanks, Flower Child." He turned and left the room, feeling her eyes on him as he closed the door.

He paused, then walked briskly down the hall.

An idea had begun to take shape during his conversation with Grace about her finding the right man. He mulled it over as he returned to his office and gathered up his briefcase.

It was a good idea.

He walked down the hall, and passed Tina, the receptionist, at her desk.

"I'll be back in a couple of hours," he told her.

Tina, a brown-haired woman in her late fifties, looked up at him.

"You look like the cat that ate the canary," she said.

Brian just grinned.

Later that afternoon, Grace left the studio where she and Will had recorded a new ad for an antique shop which was opening in town. She had a little time before going on the air, and thought she'd relax and have a snack.

She passed by the reception area. The outside door was just opening, and a tall woman entered, the wind whipping her elegant black coat around her knees. Grace got a glimpse of expensive-looking black boots and a matching purse.

"I'd like to see Brian Talbot," the woman told Tina.

"He's not here now," Tina said. "Can I help you?"

"I'm going to be one of his dates," the woman said with a toss of her head. Her hair was a white-blond shade that usually came from a bottle, but Grace saw no dark roots. Whoever her hairdresser was, she did a good job, Grace thought. She couldn't help the catty thought. Something about this woman annoyed her.

She stepped forward. "I'm Grace Norwood," she said. "I'm running the promotion. And," she added, with an enormous feeling of satisfaction, "Brian has not chosen any of his dates yet."

The blond looked her over. Grace raised her chin a notch and looked squarely back at her. Who did this woman think she was? Just because she was dressed in expensive clothes, reeked of an overpowering perfume, and looked like a sophisticated woman of the world, that didn't give her the right to assume Brian would pick her.

"He'll choose *me*," the blond said archly.

Grace heard Tina make a choking sound.

"Really?" Grace was good at controlling her voice. She was glad for the drama club productions she'd been in during high school. She made her voice questioning, slightly mocking.

The blond heard the mockery in her voice. "Yes, really." Her voice was exaggerated. Not a good actress, Grace thought. The blond narrowed her eyes at Grace, then seemed to dismiss her as someone unworthy of further thought. She turned to Tina. "I'll be back."

"Would you care to leave a name?" Tina's voice was frosty now, and Grace knew the blond's conceit had gotten to her, too. "Or your bio?"

"No." The blond, a haughty look covering her lovely face, dismissed Tina too. She turned and strode out of the building without a backward look.

"Well," Tina said as the door slammed behind the woman. "She's the worst one to come in here yet."

"You mean women have been coming in to meet Brian in person?" Grace asked, astonished.

"Yup. She's the third one in the last week. The others were bold, too, but not outright nasty. How do you like the looks she gave us? As though we were dirt beneath her feet." Tina's voice rose indignantly. "She won't get a chance at Brian if I have anything to say about it."

"And if I have any say," Grace echoed.

"I loved the way you stood up to her." Tina chuckled. " 'Really'?" She did a fair imitation of Grace.

Grace grinned. " 'Yes, really,' " she responded, imitating the blond.

They both laughed.

Grace took a piece of paper and scribbled a note to Brian.

A conceited woman was in asking for you. Tina and I feel she's nothing but trouble. I would recommend you stay away from her.
  Grace

She showed the note to Tina. "Leave this in Brian's mailbox, okay?"

"You go, girl," Tina said, with a thumbs-up sign.

Grace walked up the path to the WQNJ building early in the afternoon of the following day. She had no commercials to do today, but she wanted to tackle the new papers she was sure would have arrived from women wanting a date with Brian. She didn't want to let the stack build up like it had before. That was too depressing. No, she'd keep on top of the correspondence from now until the promotion ended.

Snowflakes swirled around her as she reached the door. Snow had been falling lightly for several hours, and was beginning to accumulate. At this rate, commuters would have a rough ride home, and she knew the station's meteorologists would be working extra hours, especially if the snow increased, as they predicted.

As she closed the door, Tina stood up from behind the desk. "Hi, Grace," she said. She held out a piece of paper. "Charles asked to see you when you came in."

"Okay," Grace said, shrugging out of her coat. Charles probably wanted to give her some instructions about frequent updates on the weather. Or maybe he had another ad he wanted her to record.

"Hi, Grace." It was Jan, one of the newspeople, on her way to the newsroom. Jan held a large computer printout in her hand. The latest weather report, Grace guessed.

"What are they predicting?" she asked.

Jan frowned. "The storm is intensifying, and it looks like we'll get more than the two or three inches we predicted yesterday."

"Keep me posted," Grace said, and entered the office she shared with several DJs. She was the only one here now. She dropped her things, including the photo and bio of Crystal she'd clipped together, on her desk. Then she went to see Charles.

Charles answered her knock with a loud "Come in!" Entering, Grace found her boss on the phone. He waved her to a seat.

"All right," he was saying. "You'd better gear up in case we have to put Operation Snowstorm into effect."

Operation Snowstorm was the nickname for the station's snow alert. If it was put into effect, people would be working overtime, handling frequent weather reports, road condition updates, and any closings, delays, or early school dismissals.

He hung up the phone. "Looks like we're getting more snow than we thought we would," he said. "I'm sure that by two o'clock, we'll have schools canceling clubs and sports."

"Probably," Grace agreed. "The roads are becoming slick."

He nodded. Then he leaned forward, beaming.

It was unlike Charles to be so jovial about an impending storm. She knew immediately that something else was on his mind.

"Congratulations on your idea, Grace. I thought it was a great one!"

Grace stared at Charles. "My idea?"

"Of course! You should have suggested it to me yesterday. Brian told me this morning."

A sense of uneasiness crept up Grace's spine.

"Which idea are you talking about?" she asked cautiously.

"The idea to find a Valentine's date for you too!"

Chapter Four

"**W**hat?"

Grace gasped, as Charles continued, ignoring her reaction.

"Finding a guy for you to date at the same time we find a date for Brian—what a stroke of genius. I should have thought of it earlier. We'll get a lot of mileage from this!'

She closed her mouth, not wanting to appear like an idiot in front of the station's owner. But Grace felt like she'd been doused with the cold snow from outside.

How could he? She had no doubt that Brian was the one who had hatched this wild scheme. Whether he'd intended to pay her back for what he thought was her crazy idea, or whether he merely meant it to be helpful after their last conversation, she didn't know. All she knew was now she was stuck with the same promotion he was—a promotion she had never liked.

She made a strangling sound, and Charles stopped and peered at her.

"You don't like the idea?" he asked.

"No," Grace declared. "I don't!"

"But it was your idea," Charles said.

She shook her head, averting her eyes. Outside the window, wind sprayed snow against the glass with a hiss. From the intercom, always turned to WQNJ, a soft ballad by the Mamas and the Papas was playing. It contrasted totally with the turmoil boiling in Grace's middle.

"It wasn't my idea." She tried to make her voice less forceful; she was afraid she wasn't succeeding. "Brian must have—" She watched as Charles's face took on a questioning note. She swallowed, then continued, "Brian must have—mistook something I said."

"Well, he's been coming up with so many great ideas since he's come on board, I guess I shouldn't be surprised. I just thought you had come up with this one." Charles smiled jovially. "But think about it, Grace. We'll get double mileage from the whole promotion. It won't mean extra work for you; Brian can sort through the guys who want to go out with you. And," he added quickly, watching her face, "if you're worried about going out with a strange man—well, we can have you meet your dates at a restaurant. Or even at the station. I know women today have to be much more careful than they did in my dating days."

"It's not that," Grace said. Obviously, Charles thought highly of Brian, his newest employee. But he'd always liked and respected her, too. "Charles, I—I'm flabbergasted. This is the first I've heard of it," she admitted.

"Well, okay," Charles said. "So maybe you didn't realize something you said would get the wheels turning. But now that Brian's suggested it, I have to tell you I think it's a great idea. I hope you'll agree to do this, Grace. If Brian can go along with it . . ."

Then so should she. Grace guessed those were Charles's next words.

And she didn't want to be a poor sport. If Brian could give in and go along with a few weeks of this silly promotion, shouldn't she do the same?

Grace cleared her throat. Then she said, "Well . . . all right, Charles. You've talked me into it." She could hear the reluctance in her voice.

"Good." Charles was smiling again. She knew he really

liked it when things went smoothly, and since he was a kind, considerate employer, Grace didn't want to let him down.

"I've got Brian working on this already," Charles continued. "Why don't you talk to him about it?"

Oh, she intended to talk to him, all right! Grace stood up, giving Charles a stiff smile. "I'll do that." She wondered if Charles heard the sardonic note in her tone.

She had a feeling he did, because for a moment, she thought she saw a flash of amusement in his expression. Then it faded. "I'd better get back to work," Charles said, glancing at the window, and he turned to the phone again.

Grace left his office, walking rapidly down the hall to Brian's. She rapped on the door, louder than usual.

"Come in." His mellow voice did nothing to calm the sparks within her.

Grace strode into the room, shutting the door behind her with a loud, deliberate, slow click. She whirled to face Brian.

Sitting at his desk, dressed in a beige sweater vest with a tweed jacket, Brian still gave an impression of height and strength.

"How could you?" Grace asked.

He smiled, his expression a mischievous one.

"I take it Charles told you about my idea?"

"Yes, he did." Why did Brian Talbot have to look so good? Why did he have that slightly spicy, masculine scent clinging to him? She pushed aside the thought, concentrating fiercely on his idea.

"How could you suggest such a thing?"

"It's what you did," Brian said, his voice calm and reasoning. "Only you went on the air."

Grace shook her head. "I just did that as a joke. You know that."

Brian had expected this reaction. Grace was staring at him accusingly, and for one tiny second, he felt guilty. Then he remembered, she'd shown only a little remorse when Charles had proposed the idea to *him*.

"It's a great idea, from a marketing viewpoint," Brian continued soothingly. "Find a Valentine date for me, find one for you—the listeners will eat it up."

It was true, and he was sure Grace knew it. "Couldn't you use someone else?" she demanded.

"Who?" he questioned.

"Well—" Grace stopped.

There really was no one else, Brian knew. Tina was married for over thirty years, Jan had gotten engaged only recently, and Alice, one of the ad reps, was going through a nasty divorce and not exactly in the mood to date. She'd said so a number of times.

Grace's face was flushed, and if it hadn't been for the anger zapping him from her eyes, she would have looked like a teenager. Her hair was brushed down again, except for the front, which was held back in tortoise-shell clips. She wore a large, aqua velour top with jeans and looked young and cute. Again Brian smelled a fruit-like fragrance. Apples, he thought. Grace was wearing an innocent apple-scented cologne.

"Still, you must have known I wouldn't like this idea," Grace continued. "I mean, I wasn't crazy when Charles suggested it for you, so why would I want to participate?"

"For the good of the station," Brian said. "I like your cologne," he added.

"My cologne?" She paused, her beautiful eyes wide. Today they looked more blue than gray. "Thanks. But back to the topic—"

"Maybe," Brian suggested, "you'd like to go along with the idea because you would like to find a special someone?"

"That has nothing to do with it," Grace protested. "When I made that remark, I was confiding in you. Not trying to start a campaign of my own!"

Brian regarded her, and realized that Grace was truly angry, not just annoyed. The mischievous spark he'd felt when he thought of the idea faded.

"I'm sorry," he said. "I thought you would be a little annoyed, but not this angry. I thought it was a good idea, and so did Charles. You seem to think it's okay to play match-maker."

Grace stopped. Her rosy cheeks paled. "I never said that," she said slowly.

It appeared he had hit the nail on the head, though. He had a strong feeling she had been doing just that. "You didn't have to say it," he said. "It seemed—well, it seemed obvious. Jan even told me you had someone you were nominating for me to date."

"Yes." Her voice was low. Abruptly, she sighed. "You're right. Okay, Brian, I told Charles you both win. You can help find me a date too." Her voice sounded resigned, and she didn't look very happy at the thought.

Why wasn't he happier about it, either? After all, it had seemed like a good idea when he'd first thought about it.

"I'll be like a big brother," Brian said. It had occurred to him that if some strange women were trying to date him, they could get some real weirdos going after Grace. And he wouldn't tolerate that for even a second. "I'll personally meet the guys who want to take you out. And I can either chaperone your dates—" Seeing a glimmer of amusement in Grace's face, he paused. "Or—you can meet the guys in a restaurant, and then go home separately. They shouldn't pick you up at your home. We don't want them to know your address."

"I guess people have to be careful today," Grace said. "But rather than chaperone—maybe we should just make it a double date?"

Brian looked at Grace. There was a definite gleam in her eyes, and Brian briefly wondered if she was feeling a little mischievous herself.

"I guess we can do that," he said. But the more he thought about double-dating with Grace and her date, the less appealing the idea was.

"Here. Watch out, it's hot."

Yadira handed a steaming mug to Grace as she entered the living room. Grace bent her head, inhaling the rich, comforting aroma of hot cocoa. "Mmm," she said, sighing, sitting beside her best friend and tucking her bare feet into the folds of her thick blue robe.

The murmur of voices from the TV, tuned to the weather channel, provided background noise as the two girls sipped their hot cocoa. Socks, Yadira's cat, was curled up on a chair next to the couch. Lincoln, Grace's golden retriever, had followed her into the living room, and now he too curled up in a favorite corner and sighed with pleasure, blinking. Though he loved their evening walks in the snow, he was just as happy now to settle down in a warm spot and snooze. Grace had been equally happy to shed her boots and wet gloves, get into a refreshing shower, and then into warm flannel pajamas.

"You seemed a little uptight when you got home," Yadira observed.

Grace nodded. "Yeah, I was." Yadira knew her well.

The two girls had been best friends since first grade, when Yadira Velez had moved into Stanhope and started school. They'd hit it off from the first day they'd met and had been close ever since. Grace's mother had laughed and said it was like having an extra daughter. But they'd spent just as much time at the Velez house, where Yadira's mother treated Grace as another family member, too. Their parents had become friends over the years, and Grace's younger brother Paul counted Yadira's brother Carlos as one of his closest buddies.

They had gone to different colleges, because Grace was studying radio communications and Yadira was going into elementary and bilingual teaching. But they had remained close, and after graduation, they'd done what they always wanted to: found jobs near each other and gotten a place together.

They had been living in the small house they rented for over a year, and though Yadira's teaching schedule meant earlier hours than Grace's afternoon and early evening shift at the radio, they usually found time almost every day to sit and chat. Evenings like this, with the snow blowing outside, were especially cozy, and reminded both friends of the countless times they'd shared sleepovers when there was a snowday at school.

That would be ending next year, though. Yadira and her boyfriend, Rafael, had gotten engaged over Christmas. Although Grace liked Rafael very much, she was aware that once Yadira got married, though they had vowed to remain close, they wouldn't see each other every day as they did now.

Grace had been filling Yadira in on all the events following Brian's arrival at WQNJ, and now she told Yadira about her day and Brian's scheme to find her a Valentine. Yadira listened, asking a couple of questions, and when Grace finished, she sat back, a serious expression on her pretty face.

"It's possible he's trying to get even," Yadira said. "Which would be childish."

Grace nodded. "He did say he thought it would help me, since I had told him about wondering if I'd find someone, too. So it's possible that his motive was just to find me someone."

"Which was his bigger motive?" Yadira asked. Her black hair gleamed in the lamplight as she bent to drink her cocoa.

Grace shook her head. "I don't know for sure. Men," she added with a deep sigh. She took a sip of the cocoa. It was now comfortably warm, and tasted sweet.

"Well, look at the plus side," Yadira said lightly. "Maybe you'll meet someone really special this way!"

Grace didn't answer, just stared absently at her favorite mug. A picture of a golden retriever decorated the side.

But she wasn't thinking about the picture. She was thinking about Brian.

Because she was beginning to fear that she *had* met someone special already—Brian.

"You know how I always believed I'd find true love?" she asked Yadira.

Yadira nodded her head. "You were right about me. When I met Rafael, it was practically love at first sight."

"Well . . ." Grace's voice trailed off. "You know, it never occurred to me that I might find someone really special . . . but he wouldn't feel the same way."

Silence greeted her.

Grace glanced at Yadira. Her friend sank back against the couch, a look of concern on her face.

"You're falling for him, aren't you? I suspected as much, the way you've talked about him constantly—"

"I don't know," Grace said. "I—sometimes I really like him, sometimes he annoys me. Falling for him? I don't know if you can say that—"

Wind gusted suddenly, throwing snow at the window. Lincoln raised his head, startled.

"Shh, it's okay, boy," Grace said. She got up and padded over to the dog, scratching him behind his ears. He sighed contentedly, gave an approving wag of his tail, and promptly went back to sleep.

She returned to the couch, where Yadira sat, studying her. On the chair, Socks hadn't moved, just lay curled up, his face buried in his fur so that he looked like a black ball.

"No, I can't be falling for him," Grace said decisively.

"Why not?"

"Because—I can't. I won't. He has no interest in me," she said. "Besides, I've been thinking of trying to get him together with Crystal. That is, if he's not like Todd." She'd told Yadira about Brian growing up in a similar town.

"I know you said you were going to bring in Crystal's photo and bio," Yadira said. "Did he see them yet?"

"Not yet, but he'll meet her." Grace drank more cocoa. "I spoke to her last night and she said she'd be home Sunday for the Superbowl. I think they'd be good together. Crystal is—well, you know. She's sweet and nice and down to earth."

"And the most practical of your siblings," Yadira commented.

"Right!" Grace continued, trying to put more enthusiasm into her voice. But oddly, the enthusiasm she'd felt originally for the idea seemed to have faded. "She's level-headed enough for Brian's taste, I think." Recalling his remarks about idealistic flower children, Grace bit her lip.

"But . . . ?"

"But what?" Grace asked.

"It seems to me there's a 'but' in there somewhere," Yadira said, smiling.

What could she say? Grace looked at her friend. "But . . ." she said, slowly, reluctantly. "I have to admit, I do like him." Her voice dropped.

Lincoln sat up suddenly, staring at Grace. He blinked at her.

Could he feel her mixed emotions? she wondered idly. She'd always thought dogs had some form of extrasensory perception.

And her emotions were certainly mixed.

"Every time I'm near the man," she began abruptly, "I feel like—well, like electrical sparks are going off all over my body. But I don't know if it's attraction or annoyance."

"Sounds like attraction to me, girlfriend," Yadira said.

"Well, maybe there's some physical attraction," Grace said slowly. "But that's all it is. Nothing more."

Yadira just looked at her quizzically.

Grace switched the topic to discussing who would be at her parents' Superbowl party, and Yadira went along with the change. Later, after Yadira had gone to sleep, Grace let Lincoln out into the fenced yard for his last run, then toweled the snow off her dog and gave him a treat. Lincoln followed her to her room, plopping down on an old comforter he used for a bed. Once again he gave his happy sigh, before drifting off to sleep.

Grace was afraid sleep wouldn't come so easily for her. Her thoughts were circling around and around Brian Talbot.

How could she feel these conflicting emotions? On one hand, she felt sparks when she was with Brian. And she wanted to know him better. On the other hand, Brian's chief emotion toward her seemed to be a mild amusement. She should probably avoid him. Plus, she knew she wanted to see if he was like Todd. Then there was the fact that she thought, logically, that Crystal might be good for him. Even if she'd lost some enthusiasm for the idea, she felt compelled to try to get them together.

Well, the Superbowl party should be interesting. Knowing the kind of multi-ethnic, multi-generational group her parents always invited, she'd felt sure this would be a good test of Brian's character. She should be able to ascertain pretty quickly if Brian was anything like Todd.

She would stay awake if she kept thinking this way. Shrugging out of her robe, Grace crossed over to her dresser. On it stood a lava lamp, almost identical to the antique one in her parents' house. Her mother had bought it for her two years ago, knowing how much Grace used to enjoy watching the blobs float in Toni's old lava lamp. Now Grace switched on her own lamp, turned off the lights, and climbed underneath the covers.

Within minutes the orange lava was floating in the cylinder. The lamp had its usual soothing effect as Grace watched it.

Why worry about Brian? Someday he'd find the right woman. If it wasn't Crystal, it would be someone else.

Maybe . . .

She averted more thoughts, and concentrated on the lamp.

Her eyelids grew heavy, and a few minutes later, she felt herself slipping into a peaceful sleep.

Grace's directions had been easy to follow, and Brian had no trouble finding the Norwood home. The house, located on a large lot on a quiet street in Stanhope, had probably once been a farmhouse. It appeared to have been expanded over the years, and was bright yellow and welcoming against the snowy landscape.

The sun was shining intermittently against thick clouds, and the day was cold and damp, holding the promise of more snow to come. Brian had hit the ski slopes yesterday, and today he found himself looking forward to the big game. And a chance to meet Grace's family.

As he approached the door, he heard barking. He touched the doorbell, and the chorus increased.

Grace opened the door. Three dogs stood beside her, barking excitedly.

She bent and held back the dogs. "Come on in."

Today she wore faded jeans and a large navy sweatshirt that said *Penn State*. Her hair was down, with no barrettes and clips, and she looked a little older—like a college student, Brian thought, instead of a high school student. Her face, as pretty as always, glowed with a happy smile.

The dogs danced around him, sniffing. He pet each one in turn—a golden retriever, a dog that he thought was a greyhound, and a smaller dog of indeterminate breed.

"This is my dog, Lincoln," she said, indicating the golden. "And my parents' dogs—April." She touched the greyhound. "And Ellie."

"Yours is a golden—I guess this one's a greyhound?" he asked, petting each dog in turn.

"Yes—my parents got April from the greyhound rescue. Ellie just showed up one day, and they could never find the owner, so they kept her." The smaller dog wagged her tail as he scratched her.

He looked up from the dogs, and saw a woman standing behind Grace.

"Mom, this is Brian Talbot," Grace said.

Mrs. Norwood's smile was as warm as her daughter's, and Brian knew instantly what Grace would look like in later years. The same height as Grace, her mother was a woman whose pretty face and welcoming smile would always make people feel comfortable. As he did, Brian realized.

She had big eyes like Grace's, although they were brown, not blue-gray. But their faces were almost identical, and though not as thin as Grace, Mrs. Norwood was slim for her age. She wore her hair down, long and wavy, past her shoulders. The color was a darker brown than Grace's, with wisps of gray winding through it.

"Welcome to our home." Mrs. Norwood extended her hand. Her voice was very similar to Grace's, mellow and warm.

"Thanks for inviting me, Mrs. Norwood." Brian shook her

hand, then gave her the bottle of wine he'd brought. "I can see you're Grace's mother. This is for you and Mr. Norwood."

"Oh, you didn't have to," she said, "but thanks! Now, don't be so formal. Everyone calls me Toni." She stepped back. "Give me your coat, and Grace can introduce you to everyone."

He followed Grace down a hall, past a dining room with a table where paper plates and cutlery were waiting to be used. They entered a large room, already half full with chatting people. A fire crackled in a fireplace, and the TV was on, showing pre-game festivities.

"This is my dad, Matt," Grace said proudly, and slipped an arm through an older man's. He was talking to another couple. "And our neighbors and friends, Rita and Ben Goldberg. This is Brian Talbot, a friend from work." She said it without missing a beat.

As Brian shook hands, he wondered why Grace's referring to him as a friend felt so good. He stored that thought away for later consideration.

Grace's father, a tall man with fair hair threaded with silver streaks, had a friendly smile. He wore jeans and a Giants sweatshirt. He looked vaguely familiar.

"Matt? Matt Norwood?" As he said the name, Brian realized why he looked familiar. "Matt 'Woody' Norwood?"

"That's me." His handshake was firm. He smiled. His eyes, the same blue-gray as Grace's, twinkled.

No wonder Grace's father looked familiar. He had been on the news a number of times, including this past November. "Woody" Norwood was known for defending the underdog, taking difficult cases where he championed the underprivileged and victims. His most recent case had made headlines all over. It involved a wheelchair-bound, handicapped woman whose husband had a long history of abusing her. She'd shot the husband in self-defense, but the husband's family had tried to make her out to be a scheming murderess. Norwood had been successful in his defense of the woman.

Brian hadn't started working yet at WQNJ when the case

was tried, so he hadn't connected the name to Grace. Now he wondered if "Woody" was a nickname from his last name, but maybe—

"Is 'Woody' for Norwood or for Woodstock?" he asked lightly.

"Woodstock," Matt Norwood replied promptly. "Although most people don't realize that."

They laughed together. "Thanks for inviting me over," Brian repeated. He meant it. He already felt incredibly at home here.

"Let me introduce you to the rest of the crew," Grace continued, "and then you can have something to eat."

"There's beer in the kitchen," Matt added.

They approached a couch, where a curly-haired young man sat, strumming a guitar. Beside him was a woman with bright-red, wavy hair.

The man looked up, and Brian knew he must be Grace's brother. He had the same blue-gray eyes as Grace and their father, and dark-blond hair. His facial features were almost exactly Matt's.

"This is my brother Donovan," Grace was saying, "and his fiancée, Renee."

They exchanged greetings. Grace turned to the last two people in the room, who were sitting on a loveseat.

"You know Will," she said. "And this is my sister, Crystal."

"Crystal Blue Norwood?" He made his voice lightly teasing.

"Yes, and you are . . ."

"Brian Edward Talbot," he said.

He observed Crystal with curiosity. She appeared to be the same height as Grace and also slim. She, too, looked a lot like their mother, but her hair was the same dark blond as Don and Matt's, and her eyes, instead of blue-gray, were brown like Toni's. Her smile was as warm as everyone else's.

Brian took Grace's offer of a beer, and sat down on the couch near Don. Before long, they were embroiled in a discussion about their favorite team's chances for winning the

Superbowl. He learned that Grace's older brother was a history teacher in an inner-city school in Essex County, and Renee taught second grade in the same city.

"Is your other brother coming?" Brian asked Grace.

"No, Paul's at college. He goes to Rutgers."

Brian got a chance to speak to Crystal during the next few minutes. Although not shy, Crystal was more reserved than Grace. She was a social worker who worked with developmentally disabled adults and their families. After a while, she and Will began talking about science fiction programs, and Brian went to get himself some snack food.

Several more people were arriving, including a young woman named Yadira, who Grace introduced as her roommate, and Yadira's fiancé and her parents.

As he went to get more potato chips, Brian passed what must have been an authentic lava lamp from the late '60s or early '70s sitting on a table. He glanced around at the group gathered in the living room and dining room. Grace's family was warm and friendly. They were upbeat, natural people, he thought, and their friends seemed to be the same.

He couldn't help comparing Grace's family to his own as he crunched a chip. Remembering his father's constantly tense look, his mother's brooding expressions except in social situations when she appeared artificially bright, Brian felt admiration for the Norwoods. Here everyone could be themselves. With the dogs and a gray-striped cat Grace called Tiger weaving in and out among the guests, everyone appeared completely at ease.

He found himself admiring the way her family treated everyone. When their neighbors, the Gordons, arrived with their son who had Down's syndrome, Grace's family greeted them warmly and Grace introduced the young man as "our friend, Tom."

"Hi, Tom," Brian said, shaking the young man's hand. "It should be a great game today."

He wished he had grown up in a family like this. His mother would have turned up her nose at many of these people, and his father would have probably ignored them. Too many times to count, Brian and his sister Lois had felt uncomfortable with their parents' snobby attitudes.

It was comforting to know that there were families who weren't so narrow-minded.

When he got up to help himself to a portion of the six-foot sub Toni had ordered, his attention wandered to a collection of photos of the Norwood children. The brother who wasn't present, Paul, was in quite a few, and though taller, he looked a lot like Grace and their mother.

There were a number of photos of Grace through the years in dance costumes. She looked adorable, and in the last one, more mature.

"Grace always loved to perform." Toni Norwood had come up behind him, and he caught the fond smile on her lips. "She took classes in ballet, tap, jazz—even ballroom dancing. Of all our children, she liked being at the center of things the best—though Paul's close."

"I guess that's one reason she's so good on the radio," Brian said, meaning it. Grace was good—very good. "And she also makes the listeners feel like old friends." Like her mother does, he thought. He pointed at the four photos hung together, of each of the Norwood kids in band uniforms. "Did they all do band?"

"Yes, they're all musicians. Donovan plays guitar and trumpet, Crystal plays flute and violin, Grace plays the French horn, and Paul's our drummer." Toni chuckled. "No surprise. In this household, music is a constant presence."

"Grace told me how you met your husband at the Woodstock concert," Brian said.

Toni laughed. "Yes, we did . . . and it was love from the start." She sent her husband a fond glance across the room.

Brian asked about Paul, and was told he hadn't decided what to major in yet. "He's still finding himself," Toni said. She sounded totally accepting of the idea.

"The game's starting!" Don announced suddenly.

Toni seated herself next to Matt, and he pulled her close.

It was amazing, Brian thought as he sat down beside Don, observing Grace's parents silently. The Norwoods still obviously cared about each other. It was almost enough to make him believe in love.

Except, of course, that he didn't. Not for himself, at least.

As the guests took seats on couches, chairs, or on the floor, Grace watched Brian with chagrin. He was seated beside Don and Rafael, Yadira's boyfriend. Not next to Crystal.

This was *not* going at all as she'd planned.

She'd carefully observed Brian when she introduced him to Yadira, her family, and Rafael. And with the Goldbergs and Tom Gordon.

Brian had acted warm and friendly with each one of them. As they discussed aspects of football, and the amusing commercials that always ran during the Superbowl, he had treated everyone with respect. There was not one iota of snobbery in his demeanor.

So, he didn't seem to be like Todd. A sudden gladness enveloped Grace. Now that she knew that, could she get him acquainted with Crystal?

She'd have to maneuver Brian into sitting next to Crystal.

She'd introduced them casually, then tried to get the two of them talking. But new people had joined the group, she'd gone to help her mom with the food, Brian had gotten something to eat—and before you knew it, Will and Crystal were deep in a discussion about the *Star Trek* movies. And her normally quiet sister was talking more than usual.

She'd have to look out for another opportunity to get Brian and Crystal talking, she decided.

She watched the game for a while, then went to get herself something to eat. Brian appeared to be glued in place, shouting when his favorite team made a positive move and groaning when the other team scored. Maybe she could get him together with Crystal when they put out desserts at halftime.

She was selecting some food when her mother entered the dining room and took a plate. For the moment, they were alone.

"Your new coworker Brian seems very nice," her mom said, helping herself to meatballs. "And he's very good-looking!"

"Yes," agreed Grace. She sighed. "I've been trying to get him to speak some more to Crystal. Don't you think she'd be a good match for him?" She selected some meatballs too, smelling the spices in the rich tomato sauce.

"Maybe," her mom said slowly. "But, Grace, I think a better match would be *you* and Brian."

"Me?" Grace dropped her fork, and it struck the wooden floor with a musical note. Retrieving it, she kept her voice low. "You're kidding, right?"

"No, I'm not. Why does the idea surprise you?" her mother continued.

"Because—I don't know," Grace said lamely. "I just thought he and Crystal might hit it off."

"I got the feeling you kind of like him yourself," Toni said softly. "And I've been watching him. I think he likes you, too."

Grace shook her head. "No, you're wrong about that. He thinks of me as a kid—he even calls me Flower Child."

"Well, even so, I think you two might be well suited for each other," her mother said evenly. "Besides," she pointed out, "it seems to me Crystal and that nice DJ Will have hit if off."

Grace was afraid her mother was right about that. Despite her efforts to bring Crystal and Brian together, Crystal and Will were the ones deep in conversation.

Grace sighed. If Crystal and Will did like each other, she certainly wasn't going to discourage them. Will was a really nice guy. The question was, who could she find for Brian?

But hours later, as she drove home, with Lincoln contentedly sleeping in the back of the car, she pondered her mother's words.

She was afraid that her mother and Yadira were right.

She was falling for Brian.

Chapter Five

Brian shuffled the papers around on his desk for what must have been the tenth time. He would never have believed that the task of finding three appropriate dates for Grace would be so difficult.

He eyed the pile of rejects with disgust. There were a lot of weirdos out there, and too many of them wanted a chance to go out with Grace. Brian had had no trouble instantly eliminating the requests from guys who said things like "she sounds hot on the radio" or "I'd like to party with Grace."

But then he'd opened a letter from one guy who had the audacity to write, "I want to take Grace to an indoor pool so I can see her in a bikini." Brian had almost choked on that one. He'd had to fight the urge to call the listener and shout "No way, buddy!"

He grabbed a black marker and drew a big X on the letter from the weirdo.

Just the thought of innocent Grace going to meet some maniac was enough to make his blood boil.

He'd never felt this protective of anyone before. Except maybe Lois.

That's it, he thought. His feelings were that of a protective brother.

He looked at the rest of the papers piled on his desk. Besides the rejects, there were also plenty of guys who sounded not quite right. Several men in their fifties and sixties had written in, and a bunch of teenagers. He went back over the "maybe" entries, rejecting one after another. He was doubtful that Grace would have much in common with a prison guard, or a toll booth collector. Maybe the owner of a landscape company—but the guy was thirty-eight. Too old for Grace.

"Brian?" Charles Armstrong's voice, accompanied by a knock on the door, broke his concentration.

"Come in," Brian invited.

Charles appeared at the door, and regarded Brian with curiosity. He closed the door behind him and slid into the chair opposite Brian's desk.

"Is that the mail from guys wanting a date with Grace?" he asked, pointing to the papers scattered on the desk.

"Yeah." Brian didn't bother to hide the disgruntled note in his voice.

Charles quirked an eyebrow at him. "Something wrong?" he said.

"There's a lot of guys who are just totally inappropriate for her," Brian replied darkly. He handed Charles a few of the letters from the reject pile. Charles skimmed them silently. Then he looked up. "You're right about these . . . I'd never let Grace go out with someone like this man who wants to see her in a bikini." He pushed the pile back to Brian. "You can toss these, as far as I'm concerned."

"I wouldn't either." Brian made a show of lifting the pile, dumping the papers in the wastebasket, and then grinding them with his foot. Grinding hard.

"But there must be some who are at least decent possibilities," Charles said after a moment.

Feeling better, Brian sat back down and eyed his boss. Charles was smiling, and Brian detected amusement in his eyes.

"What's so funny?" he asked him.

"Funny? Nothing, nothing . . ." Charles bent forward, pulling some more papers toward him. "How about this guy? He's a physical education teacher."

"Too old. He's almost forty."

"You think that's old?" Without waiting for an answer, Charles continued. "Well, what about this one? He's a golf pro."

"Sounds like a jock with no substance."

"Well, how about him?" He picked up another paper and waved it in front of Brian. "He's a college chemistry professor."

Brian reluctantly took the paper. "He might be a possibility," he said reluctantly. "But most of these guys sound pretty dubious to me."

"Why?" The question came shooting at him with the speed of sonic sound.

Brian hesitated, eyeing Charles warily. Why?

"Because none of them sound good enough for her." There. He was being honest, he told himself.

Charles was grinning again. "Maybe in your mind . . . but I think there's a couple here who Grace might enjoy meeting."

"It's not just 'in my mind'," Brian said. "I mean it, Charles. A lot of these guys sound like either weirdos or losers. You've read only a few of the letters."

"Of course we'd never put Grace in a precarious situation," Charles agreed. "But if she's meeting a guy in a restaurant, possibly at the same time you're going out, what can happen? This chemistry professor, for instance. He grew up in the area, it says, and he's a distant cousin of the mayor. He teaches at Fairleigh. That sounds innocent enough."

"He's probably the best of the bunch," Brian agreed reluctantly.

"Well, can you find a couple more possible dates? If you can't, I'll try to," Charles offered, fixing Brian with an innocent look.

Brian grabbed the papers in the "maybe" pile.

"I'll try," he said, his voice gruff.

*   *   *

"And tomorrow, Brian and I will both be going on our first dates with two people from our listening audience." Grace kept her voice well-modulated. *Control,* she thought. *Control.*

It was something she usually didn't have a problem maintaining. But today, when Charles had handed her the announcement of Brian's chosen "first" date, her heart had sunk down to her feet, and seemed to be dragging around her ankles ever since.

"Stay tuned for the announcement of the names of the lucky winners," she continued, striving to make her voice light. "We'll both be meeting our dates at the Australian Steak House! And now, a word from Australian Steak House, home of the best steaks around, served *your* way."

She cued up the commercial, and sat back, glancing out the window. The bleak winter afternoon looked as gray as she felt. She should be looking forward to an evening out with someone who sounded interesting. Instead, she found herself wishing the date was already over.

Brian had thrust a small pile of papers at her late on Monday, with instructions to pick a couple of dates from the group of men he had selected. He had handed her fifteen more e-mails and seven letters today, and after carefully going through the pile, she'd picked three men who sounded like people whose company she'd enjoy. Two of them had sent photos as well, and they both appeared to be nice-looking.

She had also given Brian her whittled-down selections of female date possibilities. She'd had a perverse desire to pick some women he wouldn't like, and had to quell the idea. That wouldn't be fair to Charles, their listeners, or ultimately, to Brian. Could she help it if she wished that her name was on the list?

At least, she thought, she'd see him outside of work this weekend.

The local hospital, which did a lot of advertising on WQNJ and hosted a health program one day a week on the air, was holding its annual Winter Cotillion this Saturday night.

Charles had generously bought tickets for everyone, since it was a fund-raiser. Most of the staff was going.

She turned her attention back to the names they'd selected.

Brian had chosen Tara, the curly-haired, sophisticated blond public relations manager as his first date.

No wonder, Grace thought, as she gazed at Tara's photo. She looked like an attractive woman of the world.

Quite different from Grace Harmony Norwood.

Grace sighed.

The next song was ready to go, and she put it on without comment. A jazzy instrumental introduction was followed by "Hello, I Love You," in the distinct voice of Jim Morrison.

When she came on again, she'd be announcing the two winners: Brian's date, Tara, and her chosen date, Jonathan. Jonathan was a twenty-six-year-old stockbroker who worked in Morristown and enjoyed appearing in amateur theatrical productions. He had written that he liked the Beatles' music, and sounded like an interesting date.

The song ended, and Grace was back on the air.

"And that was 'Hello, I Love You', one of the biggest hits by the Doors," she said cheerfully. "And now, for the announcement you've all been waiting for!" She paused dramatically. "The names of the two people chosen for tomorrow's dates, two of our lucky winners, who will be joining Brian, our sales manager, and me at the Australian Steak House, home of the best steaks around," she repeated.

She transferred her gaze to Carl, the engineer, in the next room. There was a drumroll.

"The lucky winners are . . . Tara Dayton and Jonathan Titus!"

The engineer played applause.

"We'll be meeting our dates at the Australian Steak House . . ." Grace's voice continued, almost automatically, with some details of the evening's plans. The announcement was news to their listeners, but actually, both Tara and Jonathan had been called by Charles the night before to make sure they were available.

"This will be the first of three dates we've selected from among several hundred listeners," Grace continued. "And what a great group of listeners we have! It was tough making the choice, and there was stiff competition. We finally narrowed it down to three names each."

She took a deep breath, feeling that heaviness in her heart again. "We'll be going out with those three people, one at a time, in the next couple of weeks, and for Valentine's Day, we'll be choosing one of the three for our Grand Valentine's Date." Oh no, was that a crack in her voice? Grace swallowed. She doubted it was her imagination. There *had* been a catch in her voice.

She needed to drink some water. She reached for the water bottle she always kept with her.

"Stay tuned for more announcements!" she said hastily. "And now, a number-one hit by Dionne Warwick. If you don't remember this song from years ago, you might remember it from the movie *My Best Friend's Wedding,*" she added, doing her best to sound carefree and breezy.

The song started, and Grace sat back, feeling weary, and drank some water. She hoped the catch in her voice hadn't been noticeable. Or perhaps the listeners would just assume that she was excited by the whole idea.

Excited! *Ha,* she thought. She wished Charles had never cooked up this stupid Valentine's promotion.

Grace had chosen a turquoise sweater and turquoise-and-purple skirt for the evening. The outfit was artistic-looking, and matched her slightly offbeat, unique radio persona. With gold hoop earrings and a plain gold necklace, she'd left home, feeling a little uneasy despite Yadira's encouraging "have a good time!"

She should try making the most of this weird situation, she told herself. She should simply enjoy the night out. But instead Grace found herself wishing the whole promotion was already over.

As soon as she arrived at the restaurant, she spotted Brian

and a good-looking, suave man she recognized as Jonathan from his photo. She greeted them, and after a few words, Grace and Jonathan were led to a table where Jonathan ordered red wine.

"It's a pleasure to meet you," he said easily. "I listen to your show when I'm driving home from work."

"Tell me a little about your job," Grace began, and Jonathan launched into a description of his job, his office, and his co-workers. Although he was amusing, Grace detected a hint of superiority in several of his comments.

A few minutes after their order had been taken, she observed Brian and a curly-haired blond woman being led to their table. The woman wore a leopard-print suit with a very, very short skirt. The woman's voice was husky as she said something about awful traffic on Route 206, then laughed. "Hope I was worth the wait!" she finished.

Grace strained to hear Brian's murmured, "That's quite all right."

A fireplace near their table crackled, and the woodsy smell and background of voices lulled Grace into relaxing. Jonathan kept up a steady stream of comments. Grace asked a few questions, but Jonathan did most of the talking. Every once in a while, his conversation was punctuated by hearty laughter from the woman with Brian. Grace wondered what Tara found so amusing. Was Brian amused too?

"So," Grace said suddenly, "you said you like the Beatles. Which of their songs are your favorites?"

"I always liked 'Baby, You Can Drive My Car'," Jonathan said. "And of course, there's 'Baby, You're a Rich Man' . . ." As he continued, Grace waited for him to ask what music she liked. He didn't ask.

When their dinner was served, he fixed her with a carefree smile. "You've been quiet," he said. "I guess you talk so much on the radio that you're quiet when you're off the air, huh?"

Grace had to stifle a laugh. She didn't want to annoy a listener, but really! He'd barely given her a chance to say a word.

"Actually, I'm not that quiet," she said. "You said you were in a production of 'Guys and Dolls' last summer. We did that show when I was in high school. What character did you play?"

As Jonathan expounded on his theater experience, Grace found her attention wandering. She tried to catch some of the conversation from Brian's table, but except for an occasional loud word or laugh from Tara, they were too far away for her to hear.

She really should be paying attention to her date, not wondering what Brian and Tara were talking about. With an inward sigh, Grace refocused on Jonathan.

"Of course, the dancing numbers were a challenge . . ."

Jonathan rambled on as they ate. He really could talk an awful lot about himself, and it was obvious he believed he made a fascinating topic for discussion. Her attention drifted again. What was Brian saying now? The voices at his table had dropped, and she observed Tara leaning closer.

"Well?" Jonathan asked quizzically.

Grace stared at him. "Well what?"

"I asked if you thought the musical parts of the show were difficult." A look of annoyance crossed his face, then was carefully smoothed out.

"Oh, I—I was thinking," Grace said. "I didn't find it especially difficult, I think the show we did the year after was harder."

She bent forward, sipping her soda. She'd better pay more attention to their conversation. Jonathan was, after all, one of their listeners. So she began to talk about her own musical preferences, and asked Jonathan which of today's groups he liked.

A few minutes later, when she saw Tara head to the ladies' room, she excused herself and followed the other woman.

She found Tara there, applying mascara to eyelashes that looked like they already had plenty.

"Are you having a good time?" she asked, forcing her voice to sound bright.

"Oh, yes," Tara said. "You're Grace, aren't you? That Brian—he's hot!" She smiled, turning her face this way and that as she studied her reflection. "I think I have a good shot at being his Valentine's date." She reached for her black purse, and withdrew lipstick. Pursing her lips, she applied a vibrant coral color. Her intense perfume tweaked Grace's nose.

Tara sounded as self-absorbed as Jonathan, Grace thought, as she murmured a noncommittal reply. They should have fixed the two of them up.

Grace smiled suddenly, amused by the idea. Now that would be funny. Introducing Tara to Jonathan, and letting the two of them go their way while she and Brian . . .

While she and Brian what?

Went on a date?

She had to admit to herself she liked the idea. Now that she had observed him with people outside the office, she didn't think he was prejudiced like Todd. Of course, coming from his wealthy background, he might still be on the snobby side. That remained to be seen. She'd simply have to get to know him better in order to find out.

Oh well, she told herself philosophically, *in a few days it will be Saturday, and the hospital's Cotillion.* Maybe she'd have a chance to sit next to Brian and talk to him about matters other than work. Maybe even to dance with him. . . .

Her mind conjured up an image of Brian, swaying with her on the dance floor.

She combed her hair as Tara spritzed herself with more cologne. The smell was overwhelming, and Grace sneezed.

"Oh, sorry. I sometimes overdo this," Tara said, patting her hair. "I just love this perfume. It's so sexy, don't you think?"

What Grace thought was that it was overpowering to the point of being distasteful. She stepped back, as Tara smoothed her very short skirt.

Grace tried to murmur something neutral again. But as she watched Tara move this way and that, checking herself in the mirror, she wondered if Brian would like that do-you-think-I'm-sexy look that Tara exuded.

Did Brian prefer sophisticated, bold women like Tara?

Grace realized she had no idea.

She returned to her table, feeling a little disconcerted beside Tara's blatant glamour.

Jonathan grinned. "How about dessert?" And without missing a beat he began talking again.

Grace felt relief when they finished their dessert and coffee. She could go home, and never have to date Jonathan again. He was not her idea of a Valentine's date.

He invited her to go to the movies, but she declined, explaining it was the station's policy that she should only see her date at the restaurant.

"But it's sweet of you to ask," she added graciously, with a smile. "I had a nice time, Jonathan. I hope you did too."

"Oh, I did," he assured her.

Of course he enjoyed himself, she thought, because about ninety-nine percent of the conversation had revolved around him.

Jonathan asked for her phone number, and she explained she wasn't allowed to give it out. "Company policy," she said, giving him her sweetest smile. Charles had warned her not to give out her address or phone number, and she was glad about that, at least where Jonathan was concerned. Although if he tried, he could locate her in the phone book easily enough.

As she and Jonathan got their coats, she saw Brian was still at the table with Tara, talking over coffee.

She felt as if she had stepped out into the cold even before Jonathan opened the door to the restaurant.

She thanked Jonathan again, shook his hand, and departed.

She was glad to be on her way, but concerned, too. How much time was Brian going to spend with Tara?

When she reached home, all was quiet. Yadira had told her earlier that she was tired and expected to go to sleep early. Grace took Lincoln for a long walk, and he pranced in the snow as they both enjoyed the frosty night air. The clear, dark sky with its twinkling stars helped dispel some of her uneasiness.

Once back in the house, she changed into flannel PJs and flopped down on her bed with a magazine. Lincoln sat near the bed, chewing a rawhide bone and occasionally thumping his tail. She kept thinking about Brian, and couldn't seem to concentrate on the article in front of her.

The phone rang, startling her.

"Hello?" she asked.

"Hi, Grace." Brian's husky voice seemed to flow through her like her favorite cocoa, warming her insides. "How was your date?

"Not so good," she began. "What about yours?"

"Hmmph. The same."

So he hadn't cared for sophisticated Tara!

Grace couldn't help it. She felt delighted. She pulled her pillow forward, leaning on it.

"Really?" She tried not to sound too happy. "Why didn't you like her?'

"Because she reminds me—" He stopped.

"She reminds you . . . ?" Grace prodded.

"Of my ex-girlfriend. Fiancée, to be exact."

She hadn't known Brian had an ex-fiancée. But then, she didn't know a lot about Brian.

"So you didn't care for her because of the resemblance?" Grace asked cautiously, feeling her way. This was obviously a sensitive topic.

"Yeah." There was a pause, and Grace waited, hoping Brian would fill it.

"She seems pushy and self-centered," he said suddenly, and Grace detected a bitter note in his words. "I think Tara is the kind who thinks about herself first. And always."

"I kind of got that impression too," Grace said. She was flattered that Brian had told her that much, but was curious to learn more. "We were in the ladies room at the same time, and she said she thought she had a good chance of being your Valentine's date."

"No way." His words were emphatic, and then Brian chuckled. "I have better taste than that. How was your date with Mr. Sophisticated?"

"Too sophisticated for a Flower Child like me," Grace said, trying to sound as lighthearted as Brian did right now. "To tell you the truth, I found him boring. He was so taken with himself, he could barely stop talking about his job and his interests."

"You're kidding."

"No." Then, testing for his reaction, Grace said, "I guess we should try to make better choices next time."

"You got that right." He fell silent.

Grace leaned back, huddling into the covers. "I'm glad the evening's over."

"Yeah."

"And," she continued, "I think Tara and Jonathan might have made a good combination."

Brian laughed suddenly. "You know, I think you've got something there. We should fix them up."

"Hm-hmm," she agreed. His laughter was warm and reminded her of a thick blanket, like the one she was wrapped in, on a cold winter night such as this. "And," she dared to add, "I think you and I would have had a better time if Jonathan was with Tara and we were having dinner together." There, she'd said it.

"Yeah, we could have discussed how stupid this promotion is and how annoying it is for us," Brian responded. "Maybe we can plan Charles's murder for the next time he comes up with any crazy ideas."

Grace couldn't help laughing. "Okay." But she wished Brian had said something about the possibility of them going out.

She pictured Brian, perhaps in pajamas as she was, lounging in an armchair as they spoke. She wondered if he had even the slightest wish that he'd spent the evening with her instead of Tara.

He was continuing with his idea. "At the very least, we

could kidnap Charles and brainwash him into giving up whatever scheme he's come up with."

"I'll go along with that," Grace agreed.

There was a brief pause. "Ok. I'll see you tomorrow. Good night, Grace." Brian's voice was lower.

"Good night." Grace gently placed the phone back, turned off the light, then scooted under the covers, hugging them close.

Brian had called her. She felt like an adolescent again, happy that a guy she had a crush on had called. *This is silly,* she told herself. He was just curious about her date. And he hadn't picked up on her suggestion about having dinner together.

But she found herself smiling all the same.

Chapter Six

Grace stared at herself in the mirror, turning slowly. The skirt of her burgundy cocktail dress swished against her hips. It was short without being too short, and hugged her body. She was wearing more makeup than usual, and her hair was down, to her shoulders. She smoothed her dress, the fabric silky against her hands.

She hoped she wasn't becoming another Tara, too absorbed with her appearance. But she was anxious to look her best tonight. It wasn't often that she had a chance to get dressed up, and the Cotillion was a perfect opportunity to.

And it was an opportunity to impress Brian in a nonwork setting.

She straightened her plain gold necklace, from which hung the gold peace charm her mother and father had given her years ago. It gleamed against her skin, and she had to admit it looked nice with the V neckline of her dress.

She had chosen the dress with care, wanting something flattering but not blatantly sexy. She was tired of the same old boring black cocktail dresses everyone wore. This color was different and looked good with her dark hair. She could stand out from the crowd and be a little different from the other women there.

"You look great," Crystal said, coming up behind her.

"So do you!" Grace said, meaning it. Crystal wore a navy cocktail dress that was longer than hers but had a slit up the side. It was perfect with her fair hair.

Grace had been surprised, but very pleased, when Crystal called and told her Will had invited her to the Cotillion as his date. Despite her idea that Crystal and Brian might be good together, she was happy that Crystal had hit if off with Will. They did make a nice couple. And the fact was, she liked Brian more and more and was relieved that her original plan to get him together with her sister hadn't worked.

She hadn't realized until Crystal called that she had gone out twice with Will, and they seemed to really like each other. When Crystal told her about the date, Grace had invited her to stay at her home for the weekend, since Crystal lived in Parsippany, over a half-hour away. Then they could spend some time together. Hearing about this, Will had offered to drive them both to the ball.

"You guys look fabulous." Yadira's voice came from the hall, and as Grace twirled, she saw her friend in the doorway, grinning.

"Thanks," Grace said. She had asked Yadira if she wanted to attend, but she and her fiancé were going to her cousin's engagement party that evening.

Yadira winked at Grace. "I think someone is going to be impressed."

"Yes," Crystal agreed. "Brian's never seen you dressed up, has he?"

"Only when we went to the Australian Steak House with our dates," Grace said, "and I wasn't that dressed up."

"Well, tonight you look great!" Yadira said with a laugh.

Lincoln's bark alerted them to the fact that Will must be at the door. With one last touch to her hair, Grace picked up her black satin purse and followed Crystal to the door, allowing her some space to greet Will alone.

"Have fun!" Yadira called after her.

"We will," Grace replied. Could those actually be butterflies in her stomach?

She took a deep, calming breath, and went to get her coat.

Brian entered the hotel's ballroom, scanning the crowd for familiar faces. The room, decorated in black and shining silver, was filling up already. He heard the clink of glasses and the sound of a dozen conversations, punctuated by laughter. At the back of the room, someone was warming up on a saxophone.

Normally, a charity ball would hold little appeal to Brian. His mother had dragged his father, Lois, and himself to a number of these events, and he knew from experience that if there were no people there he liked, it could turn into a long, monotonous evening.

But the group he worked with at WQNJ were fun people, not boring at all. He had found himself looking forward to tonight with a good deal of anticipation. He'd get a chance to see his coworkers outside of their usual surroundings. They could all enjoy themselves in a nonwork environment.

And he'd get a chance to speak to Grace—maybe even to dance with her—in a glamorous setting.

He'd worn his newest suit for the occasion—a dark navy suit with a pale blue shirt—and was satisfied that he looked dressed for the moment.

A waiter with a tray passed slowly by, and Brian selected a little hot dog from the offerings. He made his way through the room, as he tasted the sharp mustard and flaky pastry of the delicious hors d'ouvres.

He spotted Charles a moment later, and walked toward the group he was talking to. Was that Will with him? He'd never seen Will look so formal. Will, who usually dressed in casual clothes which verged on sloppy, actually wore a black suit, his wavy blond hair neatly combed for once. His tie portrayed the "Star Trek" spaceship.

Brian neared the group. "Will, I almost didn't recognize you," he joked, shaking his hand.

"Yeah, I clean up nice, don't I?" Will responded, laughing.

Grace's sister stood beside Will, her arm threaded through his. She looked attractive in her dark-blue dress. Brian said hello, and asked Crystal, "Is Grace here yet?"

"Over there," Crystal said, indicating a group including Tina and her husband.

He looked. The only one talking to Tina was a beautiful woman—

He looked again.

And stared.

Was that Grace?

For several seconds, Brian could have sworn that his heart stopped. And then it zoomed upward.

He couldn't believe his eyes.

The woman turned her head fully, and met his gaze. This was no Flower Child looking at him. This was a gorgeous, alluring woman.

Grace wore a clingy dress the color of red wine. It hugged her body in all the right places, and she had plenty of right places! Brian could see that Grace had a fantastic figure.

Her legs, encased in dark stockings, looked like a movie star's. She wore black heels that made her appear taller than usual. Her thick, dark hair invited his fingers to tangle in its strands as it swept her shoulders.

She walked toward him, a smile lighting her lovely face.

He took a step closer and she tilted her head, her eyes holding his. They were beautiful, blue-gray, sparkling in the lights from the ballroom. Her pert nose and perfectly-shaped face held her usual happy smile, but tonight it was more mysterious, more feminine. Maybe it was the dark red lipstick, emphasizing her luscious lips, that made him force down a sudden desire to bend forward and capture her lips with his own.

He swallowed.

"Hi, Brian," she was saying, her voice soft, enticing. Her dress swished against her body as she moved to stand next to him.

"Hi." He knew he sounded breathless. He could smell her cologne—not the innocent fruity scent Grace usually wore. This was a deeper, sensual fragrance.

"You look—gorgeous." Oh no, he sounded like a teenager.

"Thank you! You look wonderful, too," she said, her voice dropping to a husky note that sent a thrill skimming up his spine.

He couldn't stop looking at her.

"Grace . . ." Whatever he wanted to say had simply vanished from his mind.

He could hardly believe this was Grace. It was astounding that the young woman whom he'd been teasing, the one who dressed in funky clothes and looked about eighteen, was in reality a beautiful, mature woman.

As he gazed at her, his blood was racing through his veins at top speed. He could have sworn he heard a drumroll. A very primitive desire to pull Grace away from the crowded room and find a more private space tugged at him, and he had to fight it.

She smiled up at him again.

"Well, hello, you two." Charles' jovial voice broke the spell that held him, entranced. Brian wondered if Grace felt it too, this sudden awareness, this sensation that the air around them was charged with electricity.

Charles looked from Brian to Grace and back again. There was a light dancing in his eyes. "Don't you two look nice!" He turned to Grace. "Grace, I've never seen you look so ravishing. Every man here is going to want to dance with you." He turned back to Brian. "Better keep an eye on her, my boy. Someone's likely to try kidnapping her and whisking her away to a private retreat."

If anyone does that, it'll be me. But aloud Brian said, "Don't you worry, sir. I'm not going to let anyone whisk her away. I'll keep an eye on her all night." He reached out and put an arm around Grace's shoulders. Her shoulders were incredibly soft, and her cologne beckoned him.

"Of course," Charles added, appraising Brian, "there may be some women who throw themselves at you."

"I guess I'll have to keep an eye on him then." Grace returned the bantering in a light voice.

And she would, she thought.

Grace's heart had been pounding as loud as any drum from the moment she'd caught sight of Brian.

It wasn't just the fact that he looked incredibly handsome in his suit. Tall, masculine, with that certain air that made people turn their heads, Brian commanded instant respect. And attention from the women.

But that wasn't the only reason her heart was beating and musical trills moved up and down her limbs.

It was the look in Brian's eyes. The appreciative look of a man who finds a woman appealing.

Grace felt like her whole body was flushing. She was positive that Brian was feeling the same strong attraction she did.

Charles was saying something, and she struggled to focus on his words, forcing herself to look at her boss.

"—good publicity for the station," he was saying. "A lot of local merchants are here tonight—"

Her attention darted back to Brian. He was looking at Charles, and she suspected he was experiencing the same struggle to pay attention to their boss's words. As she gazed at Brian, he tightened his grip on her shoulders, and she leaned into him. It felt wonderful. Incredibly wonderful. Where his hand touched her bare skin, warmth shot into her, through her body. Straight to her heart.

She turned her head, and Brian turned his at the same time. Their eyes met.

The look in his eyes—she almost gasped.

His expression was . . . possessive. Like he felt she belonged to him.

A wave of electricity zigzagged through her whole body. Grace could almost hear the popping from the static.

". . . I'll leave you two alone," Charles was saying.

Grace turned to regard her boss. She thought she saw a look of satisfaction cross Charles's face. "I'll introduce you to the head of the hospital when I get a chance."

She murmured something. Then, taking a deep breath, she turned to look at Brian again.

The possessive expression in his eyes was still there, making every part of her sizzle.

He opened his mouth to say something, when they were interrupted again.

"Grace!" A man strode toward them. He had bright blond hair and a small mustache. "Grace Norwood!"

"Hi, Tony," she said, recognizing one of her high school classmates.

Tony's eyes were boldly assessing her. "You look great!" he was saying.

Grace introduced Brian, and felt his fingers tighten on her shoulders, which only made her tingle more.

Tony had been a popular kid in her class, voted Best-Looking Guy their senior year. Now, as Grace asked casually what he was doing, he launched into a discussion of his landscape business, which he had started after graduating from college.

"Business is booming," he said. "You should come see our office, Grace. The building is surrounded by beautiful gardens." He continued to study her.

"I'll have to stop by," Grace said. Brian had been very quiet after she'd introduced him, and now he said firmly, "Yes, we'll stop in some time."

She noticed the "we."

Tony glanced from Grace to Brian and back again.

"Okay," he said, "I'll see you soon." With one last appraising look, he left, weaving his way through the crowd, and headed for the bar, where a good-looking redhead wearing a very short black dress stood.

Grace glanced at Brian. "It was nice to see him," she said in a carefully neutral tone.

Brian looked at her squarely. "You better stay away from that guy. He's after you, and I don't trust him."

Grace couldn't help smiling, feeling a wave of satisfaction at his words. "I never really cared for Tony," she said. "He was very conceited when we were in school. He asked me out a couple of times but I always refused. And I have a feeling his attitude hasn't changed. I have better things to do than go out with him."

Brian sent her an approving look. "You're smart for your age, Flower Child." But his voice was openly teasing, and the words didn't bother Grace tonight. Because even though he'd called her Flower Child, the looks he was giving her were those of a man to a woman.

A waiter passed bearing glasses of champagne, and they took glasses and sipped their drinks, talking a little about the radio station, and some of their favorite music. Brian teasingly tried to trip her up with a few questions about rock groups and their songs, but she was able to answer every one.

The emcee asked everyone to take their seats, and Brian led Grace over to one of the tables reserved for WQNJ. They sat next to Will and Crystal.

"You look like you're having a good time," Crystal whispered.

"So do you!" Grace answered. Crystal's smile was happy, and her cheeks tinged with pink.

There were a number of presentations during the soup and salad courses, including an award to Charles for creating the health program featured on the radio once a week. Then there was a break, and the band began playing music.

Grace was sipping a soda when Brian leaned toward her. There was a gleam in his eye.

"Want to dance?" he asked.

Grace was surprised. The music the band was playing was a hot Latin cha-cha number, and she'd found most men didn't know how to do that kind of dance. But she loved to dance, and she knew her smile revealed her delight as she answered "Yes!"

Brian drew her to her feet and led her onto the dance floor. Only two other couples were there.

Brian took Grace's hands. As the music swirled around

them, the saxophone's notes hot and spicy, he slipped into the basic cha-cha step. Grace easily followed his lead.

"Know any variations?" he asked after a few moments.

"Yes," Grace said.

He turned her sideways and they did a side-to-side step for several measures. Then he returned to the basic step.

Grace whirled suddenly, stepping to the dance, and when she whirled back, Brian had done the same. Obviously, he knew the "chase" variation.

Grace laughed, and continued the I-chase-you, you-chase-me variation for another minute, before she faced Brian again.

But this time he pulled her close, doing the steps with Grace fitting neatly into his embrace.

And it felt wonderful.

After a minute, he stepped back, and Grace knew what to expect before he spun her around.

The music poured over them as she whirled, then was drawn back to Brian. Close again, then far, then closer than ever.

She was surprised to find Brian was such a good dancer. Most of the guys her age could barely make it through a slow number. Few knew the basic ballroom dances, let alone any variations.

She became conscious that a lot of people were watching them. She didn't mind being the center of attention, and was glad to have a reason to show off her dancing skills. But the best part was doing it with Brian.

The sultry music continued. Hot notes glided through the air, and Grace felt that the music and her emotions were one and the same. Heated and totally aware.

The song ended. Several people applauded, and Grace smiled up at Brian. He was grinning.

"I didn't know you could dance," she said. Brian still had hold of her hand.

"My mother made Lois and me take ballroom dancing lessons. She dragged us to a whole bunch of charity events like this one." He shrugged, as the band slipped into a slow number.

Within two notes Grace recognized "Something" by the Beatles.

"Let's dance," Brian said.

She nodded and he drew her close. And closer. She leaned her head on his chest, and he bent his head over hers.

His mom had made him attend charity balls. The knowledge caused a pang within Grace. Brian's upbringing mirrored Todd's.

Even if Brian had escaped the prejudiced attitudes and egocentrism that Todd had embraced, he really had little in common with her. He was used to a wealthy lifestyle and all the comforts that came with it. And if he ever did settle down, it would probably be with someone from a similar background.

She could feel the erratic thumping of his heart beneath her ear. Was it the last dance—or she—that made his heart beat so rapidly? She inhaled the scent of his subtle, masculine aftershave. She'd never been so close to Brian. Her fingers, on his shoulder, could feel pure male heat even through his tailored suit.

And her other hand, clasped in his, was warm. He held her tenderly, and as she moved against him in the dance, he tightened his grip.

It was wonderful being held so close to him. But it was also incredibly difficult. Was it just the slow number . . . or was it *she* that was causing him to hold her this way?

The music swelled, and Grace felt Brian's breath, stirring wisps of her hair.

She felt the smooth material of his suit pressing against her cheek. She could feel his pulse at his neck, his heart beating hard.

Did she imagine it, or did his lips brush her hair?

No, there it was again. It wasn't her imagination.

Instinctively, she snuggled closer in his embrace, and his arm tightened around her.

Enfolded in his arms, Grace felt her insides melting.

She could have stayed just like this for hours. Days. But the music ended on a melodious note, the last strains vibrating. And the emcee announced that the main course was being served.

Brian led Grace back to the table. Grace felt a little like she was living through a dream. Time seemed to stretch out, and yet the evening passed quickly. Sensations bombarded her: the delicious taste of the chicken in a sherry glaze; the smell of warm rolls; the sound of multiple conversations and flowing music. Brian's eyes met hers frequently, and each time her heart gave a little flip.

They joined in the conversation with Will and Crystal and the others at the table, but Grace didn't remember what most of the talk was about, except for the time they were naming some of their favorite "oldie" records.

" 'Proud Mary' by Creedence Clearwater Revival," Jan said.

"I liked the Tina Turner version better," someone else said.

" 'Satisfaction' by the Stones, the best rock and roll song of the twentieth century," Will contributed.

"What about 'Light My Fire' . . ." Roger began.

Brian winked, a devilish twinkle in his eyes.

Grace did notice that Will and Crystal were doing a lot of gazing into each other's eyes, and that Will's arm was often around Crystal.

Then there was more dancing. Grace and Brian got up several times, and whether they were doing an old-fashioned twist, or dancing close to a romantic tune, she loved it.

Back at the table, she sampled the chocolate mousse. The flavor was especially sweet, and lingered on her tongue.

After coffee and dessert, people began leaving.

Crystal leaned toward Grace. "We're going to leave in a couple of minutes."

She hated for the evening to end. Grace sighed inwardly, and turned to Brian.

"I have to leave in a few minutes. Will and Crystal are giving me a ride," she explained.

"I'll drive you home." His hazel eyes held hers.

A little thrill skipped up Grace's spine.

"Okay! Thanks." Quickly, she turned to Crystal and relayed the change of plans.

A few minutes later, as Grace was finishing her coffee, Crystal and Will got up to leave.

They said good-bye to those who were left at the table, and as Grace hugged her sister, Crystal whispered, "We're going out for a drink, so I won't be back to your place right away."

"Have fun!" Grace whispered back. Crystal looked very happy, and Grace could see that Will was crazy about her.

More people were leaving, and Brian whispered to Grace, "Shall we go?"

After saying their good-byes, Brian helped her on with her coat, and she gave him directions to her house.

Brian's car was a dark Jeep. Settling in the seat, Grace got a glimpse of a briefcase and a newspaper in the back.

"This is a nice car," she said as Brian climbed in. "They're good for the snowy roads."

"That's why I got it," he said, starting the car. "They can get anywhere in bad weather."

"I should get one someday," Grace said. "I like my car, but when the weather is terrible, I sometimes just stay at the station."

"You do?"

"Yes, and so do others—but only when the weather's really bad. The sofa in the staff room is also a bed, and they have a couple of futon chairs around too." She switched topics. "That was a nice party. You said your mom dragged you to things like this when you were young?"

"Yes. But," he added, glancing sideways at Grace, "I have to admit I never enjoyed a charity event as much as this one."

Grace felt a glowing warmth spread through her at his words and warm look. "I enjoyed it, too," she said softly. "More than I imagined I would."

They spoke casually about the people from WQNJ, and

Grace directed Brian to her home. They pulled up twenty
minutes later.

What would he think of her little home? she wondered.
Would it seem inconsequential compared to the places he'd
lived? He'd made no comments about her parents' home,
which was big but unostentatious.

There was one low light showing through the living-room
window of the small home she rented with Yadira. Grace
turned to Brian. "Would you like to come in and have a drink
or something?"

"Okay," he answered at once.

Lincoln barked happily as she unlocked the door. Brian
greeted the dog, who acted as if Brian was an old friend,
jumping around him and wagging his tail.

"I'll just let him out for a minute," Grace said. "Go ahead
in and sit down."

She let the dog out in the backyard, got him a dog biscuit,
and let him in again. Lincoln grabbed the treat and ran into a
favorite corner to eat it.

All the while, Grace's heart was hammering. Here she was.
With Brian. In her cozy home.

Alone.

Grace shrugged out of her coat and went back to the living
room. Brian was sitting on the multicolored couch, in the dim
light. Socks had appeared and Brian was stroking him.

"That's Socks, Yadira's cat," Grace said. "Would you like
a drink?"

"No, thanks." Brian reached out his hand and clasped
Grace's, tugging her gently. Socks stretched, and jumped on
a chair. "Come here." Brian's voice was low.

Grace allowed him to pull her, sliding beside him on the
couch. Her heart was pounding so hard she wondered if he
would hear it.

"I don't want something to drink." His voice dropped to a
husky timbre. "I want—this." Leaning forward, he pulled
Grace into his arms.

His lips came down on hers, and he kissed her. Brian's lips

were smooth and warm. Grace's heart seemed to leap into her throat, and her hands slid around his neck, feeling the warmth of his skin, the tension of his muscles. She kissed him back, and he pulled her closer, as she felt the electricity of his kiss zap her all over.

The pressure from his mouth increased, and the kiss became harder. Grace returned the intensity, kissing back just as fervently. Her thoughts whirled until she couldn't think at all. She was conscious only of this man, this kiss, this moment.

A moment which could go on forever, as far as she was concerned.

Electrical sparks sizzled through her body, igniting every nerve. She tasted coffee and chocolate. She could smell his aftershave, a scent as masculine as Brian. Her fingers instinctively stroked his neck, feeling his taut, warm skin.

His mouth left hers for a minute. "Grace . . . Grace," he whispered, kissing her cheek, her ear, her hair, before returning and capturing her lips again.

She murmured in response, tightening her hands around his neck. She clung to Brian, and he held her so tightly she thought she could feel his heartbeat.

Grace reveled in Brian's kiss. It was as if the kiss was pure energy, causing her whole body to reverberate.

Lincoln's bark penetrated the haze around her. Someone was at the door.

She pulled back, and Brian let go.

She felt dizzy, as if she was looking down from a tall cliff. As she heard voices more clearly, she tried to pull her thoughts back into her head.

"It's—it's Crystal. Or Yadira," she whispered.

Brian's breathing was labored. His tie was askew and his face as flushed as Grace knew hers was.

And the expression in his eyes—Grace swallowed.

Brian was looking at her with longing.

The door opened, and Yadira and Rafael walked in.

Grace forced herself to say hello, to speak lightly, to ignore the knowing look in Yadira's eyes. It must be obvious that she and Brian had been kissing.

Yadira and Rafael tactfully disappeared into the kitchen.

"I'd better go," Brian said, and the reluctance in his voice was tangible.

Grace stood with him. "This was a wonderful evening," she said.

An expression raced over his face—and Grace suspected Brian wanted to kiss her all over again. She could see him hesitate, and he said simply, "I had a great time too." He bent his head, kissing her lips gently—as if he was afraid that if he kissed her harder, he wouldn't stop.

"I'll talk to you soon." He lingered, then reached out and slid a finger down the side of her face, tilting it up to meet his gaze.

Even that light touch made her tingle. Grace placed her hand against his cheek, and they stood there for a moment. And another.

"Good night," he said suddenly, and turned to leave.

"Good night," she whispered as Brian opened the door. He walked to the car, paused and waved, and got in. He started the car and drove away.

Grace shut the door, then turned and leaned against it, closing her eyes for a minute.

She had never, ever experienced anything like Brian's kiss. She felt like she was glowing.

She couldn't wait to see him again.

She heard Yadira and Rafael. Collecting herself, she called good night, and went into her room, followed by Lincoln, and sank onto her bed.

What was Brian thinking right now? she wondered.

Was he thinking about her too? Was he as eager to see her again as she was to see him? As eager for their next kiss?

Chapter Seven

Brian dropped his briefcase on his desk, noting the number of pink message slips stacked there. It had been a busy Monday, and it wasn't over yet.

The station was hopping with activity, and Brian suspected that was partly because meteorologists were closely watching a strong storm that was spinning in the south. Just after his arrival at WQNJ that morning, one of the weathermen had called Charles, telling him he feared the storm was going to turn and head up the East Coast, instead of out to sea as everyone had originally predicted. Charles had been running around the station, snapping orders and calling people ever since.

All during the day, Brian had heard Vincent's updated weather reports, and now it seemed that every radio and TV station was following suit, predicting that the storm was going to take a northerly track and become a major nor'easter.

But the impending storm was probably nothing compared to the turmoil inside of him.

Before Saturday's ball, Brian had become aware that his relationship with Grace was subtly changing. She was not just a coworker. Despite her youthful idealism, he had a growing respect for Grace. She was turning into a friend.

But one look at her on Saturday and his feelings had suddenly become way too complicated.

He liked her. He liked her personality, her caring. He had even begun to admire her optimism, although he didn't share it.

And now he found himself attracted to her.

Only with Grace Norwood, Brian was afraid that his feelings were going way beyond simple attraction.

He *would* deal with it. He had to.

Starting with tomorrow night, when he and Grace were going out with their second "dates."

Grace listened to her date, trying not to look as bored as she felt.

Fred, a chemistry professor, had sounded like a nice guy on paper. And he *was* nice.

But he had little to say, unless it was about chemistry. When he got on the topic of the chemical composition of household products, Grace began to tune out.

She couldn't help comparing him to Brian. Brian had interesting things to say. He was funny. And even though he teased her, she found his comments amusing.

And there was no comparing their looks. Though Grace prided herself on not judging people by their appearances, she had been attracted to Brian from the start. He was masculine as well as handsome, with that air of confidence that made people sit up and take notice.

Fred, on the other hand, had pleasant but weak-looking features. He displayed little personality, and could have easily blended in with the wallpaper.

Added to this was the fact that at age thirty he still lived with his parents. He might be a smart man, but he wasn't independent, and he definitely didn't make her heart beat faster.

She tried again to listen to Fred's monologue, but a shrill laugh from Brian's table set her on edge.

Was he enjoying his date with the aerobics teacher?

Joanna was a statuesque woman whom people had turned to look at the moment she entered the restaurant. Nearly six feet tall, with brown hair done up in a sophisticated style, she was obviously in superb shape. She wore a purple, very clingy dress that revealed her figure as she walked. Grace had felt chagrin since the moment they were introduced. Why hadn't she "lost" this particular entry?

She wished again she had misplaced this entry as their coffee and dessert were served. Grace made herself take a deep, slow breath. She inhaled the comforting aroma of freshly-baked apple pie and coffee. Soon, this date would be over, and she could go home, she told herself.

Home, to wonder if Brian had enjoyed himself with Joanna.

As she had with Tara, she excused herself when she saw Joanna heading toward the ladies' room.

Unlike Tara, Joanna wasn't preening before the mirror. She seemed less caught up in herself. Grace wondered if Brian would find her appealing. Joanna said little as she applied lipstick.

"Having a good time?" Grace asked, fumbling for her own lipstick.

"Oh, yes," she said breezily, powdering her nose. "He's a very intelligent man. He looks like he's in good shape too." Joanna turned, studying her reflection. "How about you?"

Next to Joanna, Grace felt like a shrimp. "Oh, fine," Grace said. Did Brian like tall women? she wondered.

She looked at her reflection. She knew her face was attractive and that she had a nice figure. Still, compared to Joanna, Grace felt decidedly unglamorous.

Back at her table, Grace finished the rest of her coffee and ended the date, telling Fred she had to run to the grocery because of the impending storm. He didn't question her, just thanked her for the date. Brian and Joanna were just getting up from their table when Grace scooted out of the restaurant. Just seeing Brian talking to Joanna made the ache inside her grow.

The storm was expected to hit sometime tomorrow. Grace drove to the nearest superstore and parked.

The place was jammed with people piling everything in their grocery carts from the usual bread and milk to bottled water and flashlights. The bright lights and unusual noise level verged on irritating as Grace pushed her cart. Despite the fact that every single register was open, the lines were long.

Grace briskly dropped things in her grocery cart. Diet soda, cocoa mix, flashlight batteries. She turned a corner.

"I guess you're here for the same reason I am."

Brian's voice! She stopped.

Grace whirled around. Brian was a yard behind her, pushing a cart and grinning.

"I decided to get a few things before the storm hits," she said. "You, too?"

"Uh-huh. You've lived in this area all your life. I'm a former city boy. What do you recommend I get?"

Grace ran down a quick list of essentials, like canned foods in case the power went out, batteries for radios and flashlights, and candles.

"Do you have a manual can opener?" she asked.

Brian fell into step with Grace. "Yeah," he replied, following her suggestions and adding two flashlights to his cart.

A short woman who looked at least eighty whisked by, a determined look on her face. "Excuse me," she said loudly, nearly plowing into another shopper.

Grace gave him an amused grin as she stepped out of the old lady's path.

Brian watched Grace, wondering what else she would buy. She selected dog food and treats and dropped them into her shopping cart. She obviously wanted to make sure her dog was as comfortable as she was.

She paused, and selected some cat food too. "In case Yadira didn't get to the store today," she said. "I haven't seen her since last night and I don't know if she has extra."

A man hurried by, pushing a cart that screeched.

"Did you have a nice time with your date?" Brian asked, as casually as he could.

Grace glanced at him. "It was all right," she said. He couldn't read her expression.

"He seemed—nice," Brian probed, wishing he didn't care so much what she thought of the brilliant chemistry professor.

Grace laughed. "Nice enough. I just find it hard to believe a thirty-year-old-guy is happy living with his parents. You'd think he'd want some independence."

Grace hadn't cared for Fred! A surprising rush of relief flooded over him.

"I'd hate to still be living with my parents," he remarked.

"I love my parents, but I like being independent," Grace agreed, picking out some instant hot cereal. "So, how was your date? She was very attractive."

Brian shrugged. "She is, but she isn't my type."

"Oh?" Grace met his eyes.

"No, she was . . . too pushy," he said. "Halfway through the meal she was inviting herself over to my place to give me a massage."

"Really? I'm surprised you didn't try it," Grace said. Her face, always so candid, looked amazed.

There was only one woman who Brian could imagine giving him a massage—and it wasn't Joanna.

"I wasn't interested," he said, then grinned down at Grace. "If, on the other hand, *you* want to give me a massage . . ." He gave her a deliberately suggestive look.

Grace laughed. "I might just try that sometime," she retorted.

"Of course, then I'd be glad to return the favor anytime."

She turned pink, for once seeming to be at a loss for words. Then she said, "Well . . . maybe sometime." She turned to look at the aisle they were in, and grabbed for some bread. Brian had a feeling it was more to avoid the conversation than because she needed to buy bread.

"I'm done," she said, reaching for fruit-flavored yogurt.

"So am I," he said.

They got into a line, and proceeded slowly through the checkout. Brian helped Grace load things into her car, then waved good-bye and pushed his cart toward his Jeep.

As he drove home, his mind couldn't help conjuring up images of Grace massaging his shoulders. . . .

"That's it for today's Love, Peace, and Happiness Hour," Grace said, as the last notes of Santana's "Black Magic Woman" faded away. "Stay tuned for national and local news, and an up-to-the-minute weather report. And remember, the roads are bad, so stay home and keep tuned to WQNJ!"

She sat back as the engineer played the theme song for her special show, then heard the news come on. Taking off her earphones, Grace stretched.

The storm was raging outside. It had begun as thick flakes late in the morning, and quickly turned into a wind-driven heap of snow. Already, at 6:00, they'd probably gotten over eight inches, and it was officially being called a blizzard. And it was supposed to snow all night and into the morning. Her afternoon time at the mike had been interrupted by frequent weather updates and road condition reports, plus plenty of early school dismissals and activity cancellations.

Normally she'd be on right after the news, but she and Will and Dennis, a night DJ, had agreed to make some changes in their schedules. Grace and Will were going to help Dennis out in case Liza, the late-night DJ, couldn't get into the station. The morning DJ, Roger, was already there, planning to sleep over, so he'd be present for his 5 A.M. shift.

With Will going on next, Grace had a break, and then she'd be on for a few hours while Will slept. She'd packed sweats for sleeping, a pillow and blanket, and clothes for the next day. Yadira was taking care of Lincoln while Grace stayed at the station.

She left the studio and went to the staff room to get the microwaveable meal she'd brought with her, and a sample of the minestrone soup which Tina had brought in for everyone.

The delicious aroma of vegetables and spices met her when

she opened the staff room door. Will was finishing his meal, and Roger was helping himself to soup. Dennis was sprawled out on the couch with a magazine.

Everyone greeted her.

"I just spoke to your sister," Will told Grace, beaming.

"How is she?" Grace asked, taking her meal out of the refrigerator. "I haven't spoken to her since Monday."

Grace had talked at length to Crystal on Sunday, and again Monday. Her sister had confided that she thought she was in love with Will.

"I know it's sudden," Crystal had told her, "but I think This Is It."

Grace was genuinely thrilled. Will was a really nice guy, and he obviously cared for Crystal. She had never considered fixing them up. But fate had stepped in, and now she hoped things worked out for them.

"Crystal's okay. When I called she had just gotten in. She left work early but the roads were bad. I told her," Will continued, "to stay home tomorrow. It's going to be a mess out there." His face wore an expression of concern.

"I'm sure she will. In fact, a lot of places will be closed," Grace said, popping her meal into the microwave.

She talked to Will, Roger, and Dennis while she ate. She sampled Tina's hearty soup, all the while wondering what Brian was doing right now.

And then, as if she'd given him a cue, the door opened, and Brian strode in.

Grace almost gasped. What was he doing here? Her heart went from a slow and steady beat to a rapid rhythm. Quickly, she drank some of her diet soda.

"Hey, what are you doing here?" Dennis asked, echoing Grace's thoughts.

"The roads are terrible," Brian said. "I've been getting a lot of paperwork done in my office. I thought I'd stay here and help everyone out." He turned to look at Grace. "If you absolutely need to get home, Grace, I'll drive you. I have four-wheel drive."

Pleasure shot through Grace. Brian was worried about *her!* It was so sweet. And the fact that he was here to help out— it was obvious that Brian was a team player, a person who cared about others and was willing to pitch in.

"That's so nice of you," Grace said. Could Brian see from her expression how impressed she was? "I'm staying here tonight with everyone else. But we might be able to use your help."

"Yeah, the engineer's going to need a break," Will said. "We're going to be taking turns covering for him, but we can always use some assistance. Do you know anything about engineering?"

"Yes," Brian said, sitting down at the table. Grace was surprised. He'd never mentioned it. "On my first job, they taught me some simple stuff for emergencies like this one. If you get a stack of music ready, I can cover for the engineer."

"We might need some help manning the phones, too," Roger added.

"No problem." Brian went to the refrigerator, took out a brown bag and a Coke, then helped himself to the soup. He sat down beside Grace, and she watched as he pulled out a large sandwich.

"Hey, you two looked pretty good on the dance floor Saturday," Will said.

"Thanks," Grace murmured, pleased. She glanced at Brian.

He looked pleased himself. "Yeah, I think we did." He grinned at Grace. "Our Flower Child is multitalented."

"I like dancing," Grace said. *Especially with you,* she thought.

"So do I." Lights danced in Brian's hazel eyes. Then he turned to Will. "You looked like you were having a good time too."

"Yeah, I was." Will smiled at Grace. "Your sister is the best."

"Was that Grace's sister you were with?" Roger asked.

They spoke for a while, then Will left to go on the air. Jan came in, curled up on the couch, and gave them the latest weather update, which showed the storm had stalled over the area.

"We may be here for a long time," she said wearily.

The phone began ringing, and the next few hours whizzed by. Grace and Brian answered the phones for a while, taking down notes, and verifying them, about school closings for the next day.

As they worked together, Grace was conscious of an incredible sense of camaraderie. It was as if she and Brian had been friends for a long time, working on projects like this. Within minutes they had developed a rhythm to their routine, and things were going as smoothly as they could, given the blizzard.

Later she took another shift on the air, having a little fun with some summer songs to offset the howling wind and snow outside. She played "Summer in the City", "Hot Fun in the Summertime," and "In the Summertime" while Jan, then Brian, brought her updates on road and weather conditions.

During a Beach Boys song, she found herself gazing out the window. Snow blew against the glass, making a hissing sound, and the window rattled. She could barely see the plow going by outside, its lights fighting the snow and wind.

But inside WQNJ, it was warm, and she felt good.

"And that was the Beach Boys with 'Surfin Safari'," Grace said. "Stay tuned for news and an updated school closing list. And LaShone and Maritza, if you're listening, we have an announcement about *your* school district coming up!"

She took off her earphones, and Dennis, who'd been watching from the engineering booth, got up to take over.

She was done for the night. Grace stretched and yawned, then went to her office to get her things and change to her sweats.

After changing, she entered the staff room. Now, only one small light glowed. One couch was opened up, and Will was sleeping on it, ensconced in a large plaid sleeping bag. On the other couch, Jan was stretched out, also in sweats, her head on a pillow and a yellow blanket tucked around her. Roger lay in a sleeping bag on the floor, fast asleep.

Brian, now dressed in navy sweats, was in the large reclining chair, and Grace thought he was sleeping, until he unfurled his long legs and stood up.

"Do you want the chair?" he whispered, coming to stand beside her.

Grace shook her head. "I'm not ready to go to sleep yet."

"Me neither. Will told me they'd wake me early, but so far I haven't been able to sleep."

"I'm going to make us some hot cocoa," Grace whispered. "We can go into the reception area, so we don't disturb anyone."

She tiptoed over to the stove, heated water, and made two instant cocoas. After silently handing a mug to Brian, they left the room, closing the door quietly behind them, and walked down the corridor to the reception area.

Only one dim lamp was on. A large jar candle was lit on another table, and warm vanilla scented the air. It was cooler here, where a draft crept in from one of the front windows. Grace grabbed the forest green velour blanket draped over one arm of the couch, and curled up in a corner of the sofa. Brian sat down next to her. She inhaled the rich scent of the cocoa, before sipping. The hot liquid was sweet and slid down her throat, the smooth mug warming her fingers.

Outside, the wind gusted, throwing snow at the window behind them, which rattled loudly. The radio, always turned to WQNJ, was on low. Dennis was playing a medley of Elvis tunes.

It might be this winter's worst storm outside, but here inside there was a sense of peace. Grace huddled down into the comforter, sipping her cocoa. Sitting here with Brian was unbelievably cozy.

Strangely, he echoed her thoughts. "This is . . . nice," he said, meeting her eyes. "Everyone here is like family. It feels like home."

"We are like family," Grace said quietly. "I bet you couldn't find a more loyal group at any other radio station."

"It wasn't like this where I used to work. People were competitive, cut-throat types there." Brian sipped his cocoa. "This is good."

"Yadira and I always shared cocoa or hot chocolate in this kind of weather," Grace said. "Our mothers made it when we were little, and when we got older, we'd make it ourselves. It's still a ritual with us on cold winter nights, sharing a hot drink and talking."

"You're lucky you have such a close family, and close friends."

Grace heard the note of wistfulness in his voice, and her heart seemed to bend in her chest. She could feel the weight of personal pain belonging to Brian.

"It sounds," she began cautiously, "like you didn't have a very warm family."

"No, I didn't." Brian sighed, and drank again. Grace was silent, hoping he would go on. She was not merely curious; she really wanted to understand Brian. And perhaps talking about his past would be good for him.

He filled the silence suddenly. "My father and mother always treated Lois and me well," he said. "They loved us. But my parents didn't get along with each other. My father traveled a lot—he was a corporate executive for a large company—and sometimes he was gone for weeks at a time. When he was home, he and my mother fought. Constantly. I have no idea why they ever got married," he added abruptly. "They never seemed well-suited. As I got older, it seemed to me that one of the reasons my father liked to travel was so he'd have an excuse not to be around."

"That must have been difficult for you and Lois," Grace said evenly.

"Yeah. We missed him, and yet it was more peaceful when he wasn't home. My mother wasn't so uptight. When he was home, she'd be yelling, he'd yell back, and there were arguments almost every day. It was unpleasant." He met her eyes.

"Not exactly the kind of atmosphere a kid wants to come home to."

"I don't blame you," Grace said softly. "Did they ever consider divorce?"

"Not that I know of," Brian said. "They must have cared about each other once, but—sometimes I think they couldn't stand each other. Maybe they didn't believe in divorce."

"I guess that's why . . . why you don't believe in love." Her voice dropped. Her fingers stroked the velvety blanket.

"That, and—" Brian stopped.

"And . . . ?" Grace waited.

Another chilly draft crept through the window. The candle's flame flickered, sending shadows careening around the wall. Grace clutched at the soft cover, wishing Brian would pull her into his arms. She said nothing, sensing he was about to confide in her.

He was silent for a minute. Then, slowly, he began to talk. "And . . . what happened with Victoria."

"Was she your—fiancée?" Grace asked.

"Yes." His face had taken on a brooding expression, his brow furrowed.

"What happened?"

He turned to her suddenly. "I met Victoria in one of my classes. I was a senior, she was a junior. She was tall and gorgeous, with long blond hair—" He stopped, his eyes taking on a far-away expression. "I fell for her like a ton of bricks. She was beautiful and bright and we had a great time together. For the first time in my life, I thought that maybe my parents' marriage was a fluke. Maybe there really was true love in the world."

Grace's heart grew heavy, with a horrible achiness inside. She had a feeling she knew what Brian was going to tell her.

"Go on," she said, her voice just above a whisper.

"I got serious. After my graduation, I started talking to her about marriage. She said she wasn't sure, she wanted time. So I gave her time. We didn't get to see each other that much in the next few months. I was working at my first job, and she did some traveling with her family that summer. Then, in the fall, she was back in school, busy with classes. Or so I thought." His face darkened, and Grace could hear the tension in his voice. "Finally, I pushed her to get engaged. Then she told me the truth."

Brian paused, taking a deep breath. "She came over to my place. And she told me she'd started seeing—" Again he paused."—another guy."

"Oh, no," Grace whispered. She wanted badly to reach out and touch Brian, to erase some of his remembered pain. But she stilled her hand, wanting him to finish, to get out the whole story.

"Victoria had come from a family like mine—a family where her parents didn't get along. But hers was worse than mine. Her father had had numerous affairs, and her mother did too, but she stayed married because she wanted the security. Victoria's father was a wealthy businessman. That's why it had seemed like a miracle we found each other—two people who didn't believe in love, had found love." Now Brian's mouth turned into a grimace. "Only it turned out I was the only one who had started to believe in love. Victoria had no such illusions. She said she loved me, but I don't believe she did. She was looking for security, plain and simple. And she found it."

Brian turned to Grace, his expression dark. Grace couldn't suppress a shiver. He put down his mug.

"She'd met this medical student. He was doing his residency, specializing in heart problems. Hearts! Hah!" Brian's tone turned caustic, seeming to scrape against Grace's skin. "Victoria knew he had a brilliant future and would make a lot of money. She left me for him, and they got engaged. A year later I saw their wedding announcement in the *New York Times*." The bitterness in his voice swelled, filling the room.

"Oh, Brian." This time, Grace didn't resist the impulse to touch Brian. She placed her mug on the table, then reached out, covering his hand with hers. "I'm so sorry. It must have been a terrible time for you."

He mumbled "uh-huh," gazing at the wall.

"She sounds like a very selfish person," Grace continued. Brian's hand was cold.

"What?" He turned to face her again.

"I said, she sounds like a very selfish person. She had fun with you, then dumped you to marry for money. Obviously she was very shallow too." Grace heard the indignation in her own voice. "She was looking for money, not love. You're better off without her."

"I know that now," Brian said, his voice less bitter. "But seven years ago, I was barely an adult, just twenty-two years old. It hurt like hell."

"It must have been awful."

"I lived," he said suddenly, and Grace detected a note of typical male pride in his voice. She knew from her brothers that men would minimize their hurt, unwilling to admit how badly their feelings had been trampled.

"Yes, you did," she agreed, her voice soothing. But he was living with a fear of love, Grace thought, realizing she had just discovered the *real* problem. It wasn't just that Brian didn't believe in love. He knew he could love. It was that he was afraid of love, afraid of the heartache it sometimes caused.

Afraid of being hurt again.

Brian stared down at her hand, as if just becoming aware it covered his. He turned hers over. His had begun to warm, and he squeezed hers lightly.

Then he withdrew his hand.

Her own hand felt bereft and cold.

"Now you live with the feeling that love isn't possible." Grace said the words gently. She didn't mention the fear. "That's a sad way to live."

"But it's realistic," he said.

"No." Grace shook her head. "It's not. There *is* love in the world. Look at my own parents. And Charles and his wife. Will now, with Crystal . . ." Her voice dwindled, as she caught a sudden flash of amusement in Brian's face.

"You're impossible, a hopeless romantic!" he declared, shaking his head. But she'd gotten him to smile.

"Maybe." She tried to keep her voice light. It was obvious that Brian didn't want to dwell on his pain. And although her heart ached with sympathy, Grace knew he wouldn't want her to get all teary-eyed.

"Maybe," she repeated, "but I'd rather be like this than— than cynical."

"Didn't you ever get disappointed or hurt by a boyfriend?" he asked.

Briefly, Grace told him about Todd.

Brian listened, nodding. "You were smart to get out of the relationship before it went further. But you could get hurt someday," he warned.

"I hope not. But if I do, I'll survive. Like you," she added.

Brian stared at her for a moment. Then he leaned over and gathered Grace and the blanket into his arms.

"I hope you don't get hurt, Flower Child."

His breath stirred her hair. Grace had to fight sudden tears. Despite Brian's own suffering, he was still thinking of others. He was thinking about her.

"I'll be fine," she said, her voice scratchy. Instinctively, she put her arms around him and cuddled into Brian, hearing his heart thumping near her ear, feeling the warmth he generated. His arms held her gently.

They sat quietly for a few minutes. The beat of Brian's heart was steady, and ensconced in his arms, Grace felt warm and cozy.

Slowly, she felt the tension easing out of Brian's muscles. His breathing slowed. When she felt him totally relax and knew he had fallen asleep, Grace closed her eyes.

This was wonderful. Snuggled next to Brian, warm and sleepy, with the storm blowing outside, she felt unbelievably comfortable.

Her last thought before sleep overtook her was that she could stay like this for hours . . . every night. . . .

* * *

A sudden, fierce rattling of the window woke Brian.

There was something warm clinging to him. A soft, incomprehensible murmur sounded near his neck.

He opened his eyes, and it took him a few moments to realize where he was and why he felt so nice and warm and cozy.

A dark head was burrowed in his shoulder. Grace. She was tangled in the blanket with him, fast asleep.

The room was almost dark. The candle flickered, sending out scented vanilla smoke. A small digital clock on the table said 1:15 A.M. The radio was silent now, and would be for about four hours.

The two of them had fallen asleep on the couch. His legs were stretched out, and Grace was curled up next to him, a ball of cuddly warmth under the soft blanket. Their arms were around each other, the blanket surrounding them.

Brian felt refreshed, as if his short sleep had been peaceful.

He moved his head so he could look at Grace. Even devoid of makeup, asleep, her face was beautiful. She looked content and undisturbed, as if she hadn't a care in the world. But she was snuggled close to him.

She was so naive, so trusting. It almost hurt to think that she would someday experience disappointment and heartbreak. What if some man hurt her much worse than Todd had? The thought made his gut clench.

And yet, Brian had come to recognize that Grace was strong enough to weather hardships thrown her way. With her positive attitude she'd survive.

And she just might find the man of her dreams, who would be crazy about her—

Some guy who would be damned lucky to find that Grace Norwood loved him.

For just a second, Brian wondered what it would be like if *he* was that lucky man.

He buried his face in her hair. Holding her close, he felt wonderful. He inhaled the innocent fruity smell that clung faintly to her. He let his fingers glide through her hair. It felt like strands of satin. It would be so easy to imagine that he was her lucky boyfriend. . . .

After a moment, guilt pricked the edges of Brian's mind.

It would never happen. He must not let Grace fall for him.

Because she'd only end up with the same heartache he'd once felt. The pain of loving someone who didn't—or wasn't capable of—loving back.

And he would never deliberately hurt her.

No, he told himself firmly, he'd better put some distance between himself and Grace. Before she impulsively fell in love with him. Before it was too late.

He pulled back, gently untangling himself from her hold.

That simple act was much more difficult than it should have been.

Moving to the other corner of the couch, he repositioned himself so that he got some of the blanket.

He felt much colder than he had before. He closed his eyes, and waited to drift back to sleep.

Why did he feel so strangely alone?

Grace woke up during the night. A draft was blowing from a corner of the window, and she shivered.

Sitting up, she saw Brian sleeping at the opposite end of the couch, and it looked like he had taken most of the blanket with him. He must have moved during the night, because she could remember falling asleep in his arms. Maybe he'd been uncomfortable, squeezed into the corner of the couch. Now he was stretched out.

She tugged on the blanket, and when she had half of it, settled down to get some more sleep.

Several hours later, she heard movement nearby, and opened her eyes to see Roger passing her on the way to the studio.

She drifted back to sleep, but by 6:30 people were moving back and forth, and she woke and sat up.

Brian had disappeared.

The storm did not abate until late in the morning, but everyone was awake and pitching in with work by 7:00. They reported on school and building closings, road conditions, and weather updates. At one point people were moving their cars as the radio station's parking lot was plowed out. Brian moved Grace's car since she was taking a turn at the mike.

By afternoon, the rest of the staff was able to get in, and they switched schedules around further so everyone who'd worked late and slept at the station could get off early.

When Grace ended her shift in the early afternoon, Charles told her to go home, he'd get Liz to cover her show.

She was reluctant to leave, despite the fact that she was tired. And she knew her reluctance was because of Brian.

They had gotten closer last night. And not only because they'd spent part of the night with their arms around each other—although that had been amazingly comfortable.

Their closeness had come from sharing their emotional experiences.

His confiding in her about his past had been illuminating. She understand him better now.

And maybe he understood a little about her.

But she also knew enough about men to realize that Brian would probably be embarrassed that he had told her so much, and wouldn't want to discuss his broken heart any further.

It was no wonder he was so cynical about love. His parents' poor example plus his own experience had combined to make him reluctant to believe any relationship could work for him. His old girlfriend obviously gave no thought to the feelings of others. She was a simple social climber. It had been Brian's bad luck to meet her, and because of his youth, he hadn't realized her true character and had fallen for her. Victoria must have done a great acting job, pretending to be a warm, caring individual. But in the end her true colors had been revealed.

Would Brian ever take a chance on love again? Grace wondered, entering her office and sitting down at her desk. If she was in his position, she supposed she'd feel reluctant to get involved again.

But maybe he would get involved. Maybe he just needed some time.

She knew Brian would scoff and say she was being overly optimistic.

She couldn't help it. She was optimistic, hoping that next time, for Brian, things would be different.

For Brian and . . . her?

The following day Grace arrived at the station before her usual time. After the crazy schedule caused by the blizzard, she'd been happy to get to sleep early the night before. Brian had occupied most of her dreams, but she'd woken up feeling rested and hopeful. And now she was raring to go.

She had to prepare for an upcoming "Around the Town," a weekly program featuring interesting people and events in the area. She would be filling in for Dorothy, one of their part-timers, in a few days, interviewing a local poet who had just won a national award. Dorothy usually ran the program, but was on vacation right now. And she and Brian were supposed to pick their third dates.

Most of all, she found herself looking forward to seeing Brian.

Their conversation yesterday before they left the radio station had been brief. Brian was cooler than he had been during the night, and Grace knew her instincts were correct. Brian had been embarrassed that he'd confided so much in her.

She had gone along with his superficial conversation, acting as if nothing much had happened, as if she didn't know about the heartache he'd dealt with.

Now she went to the receptionist's desk to check her messages. As she rounded a corner, she heard a voice which sounded familiar.

". . . not in again?" the woman was saying.

The smell of industrial-strength perfume reached Grace.

Grace entered the reception area. She instantly recognized the tall blond woman who stood by Tina's desk. It was the woman who had come in once before, wanting a date with Brian.

"No, and I don't expect him back this afternoon," Tina replied firmly. "He said he had a number of appointments out of the office today."

"Hmph," the woman said under her breath.

"Can I leave him a message?" Tina asked, her voice as cold as the packed snow outside.

Grace couldn't help smiling. Tina didn't like this woman any more than she did.

"Tell him his next date was here," the woman shot back, tossing her head. She grabbed the luxurious looking gloves she'd placed on the desk, and walked out, holding her head high. Her petulant expression marred her classic features.

"Have a nice day," Grace said in a syrupy voice.

The woman shot her a nasty look, and Grace knew she'd recognized her too-sweet tone as sarcastic.

The woman slammed the door as she left.

Tina laughed. "I loved the way you said that."

"She's conceited, isn't she?" Grace said, smiling. "And she doesn't give up."

"No, she doesn't," Tina said. "I don't like that woman. She's got a lot of nerve."

"I guess she really wants a date with Brian," Grace said. She had to force herself not to sound wistful.

"Well, the Blond Bombshell isn't going to get one if I have anything to say about it," Tina said firmly. "Brian doesn't need that type of woman."

"What type do you think he needs?" Grace asked, as casually as possible.

"Someone who's lively, but warm and sincere on the inside. Someone like . . . you."

Grace felt her cheeks grow warm. Obviously there was some speculation at the station about her and Brian. It must have been the way they danced at the hospital's cotillion.

"I wanted to fix him up with my sister," Grace said. "But Crystal ended up going out with Will."

"So I've heard," Tina said, a bright smile covering her face. "Will was talking about her the other day. He seems to be crazy about her. I'm happy for him. He's a nice guy, don't you think?"

"Yes," Grace agreed. "They seem very happy together. By the way, that soup you made was delicious. You'll have to give me the recipe," she said. "Any messages for me?"

"Just this." Tina handed her a pink message slip.

It was a brief note from Brian. He'd chosen his third date, and asked if she would select hers.

Grace tried to remain nonchalant, but inside she felt like her heart was taking a slow elevator downwards.

"I'll see you later," Grace told Tina, and escaped to her office.

From the moment she saw Brian's third date, Grace's heart sunk further.

It wasn't her looks. Joyce was attractive, but certainly not gorgeous. Of average height and weight, with medium-brown hair, she was the kind that could go unnoticed in a crowd. Except for her smile, which was sincere and dazzling. It lit her whole face.

Grace knew instantly that Joyce was a nice person.

A kindergarten teacher in the nearby district of Great Meadows, Joyce was a twenty-seven-year-old woman who had been widowed after only a few years of marriage. Since her husband had died in a car accident two years ago, she had not dated; but she'd written that she thought going out with Brian would be a nice, unpressured way to ease back into the social scene, which she thought she was ready for now.

And Grace could tell, as they talked briefly in the lobby of the quiet continental restaurant, that Joyce was sweet.

Her heart grew heavier.

Joyce was just the kind of woman she'd pictured for Brian at the start of this whole Valentine's campaign. Someone who'd be patient and kind and slowly lead him back to the realization he could fall in love.

Joyce could be that woman. She could be somebody he would love.

Grace felt an achiness inside.

"Hello, ladies. Is one of you Grace Norwood?" a voice said from behind them.

Grace turned. Her date, a tall, hefty man with auburn hair, had the same pleasant look he'd had in his photograph. Lewis was a twenty-eight-year-old environmental engineer. He'd written that he'd spent a lot of years in graduate school, with little time to do anything but study. But now, with his Ph.D. finished, he was working and enjoyed meeting different people.

"I am," Grace said, and did her best to concentrate on Lewis.

Brian arrived right afterward, and though she was talking to Lewis, she could see Brian smiling and talking to Joyce.

Lewis turned out to be a nice person, neither self-centered like Jonathan nor boring like Fred. He had a congenial way about him, and Grace found herself enjoying their conversation. They talked about music and the environment, and several times Lewis made Grace laugh with his amusing comments.

He might be someone I could like, she told herself.

Except, of course, that she kept comparing Lewis to Brian.

After their main course, she excused herself, and Joyce joined her in the ladies' room a few minutes later.

"Are you having a nice time?" Joyce asked as Grace brushed her hair.

"Yes, he's . . . nice," Grace said. She heard the little catch in her throat. "How about you?"

"Oh, Brian's very nice. I like him," Joyce confessed. Her smile was wide and her eyes sparkled. "I feel like I'm no longer afraid to date. I could go out with him again." She touched a dark-pink lipstick to her lips.

Something twisted inside of Grace. "That's good." She managed to keep her voice even.

When she returned to her table, she found Lewis standing by Brian's table.

They both turned to her.

"Lewis suggested we all go for a drink together," Brian said, regarding Grace. His eyes were serious, and she detected a cautious note in his voice. "He knows the rules, that we're not supposed to go anywhere alone with our dates, but he figured a group drink would be okay at the bar here."

"If it's okay with you," Lewis added, "and with Joyce."

Grace hesitated. She guessed that sitting in a foursome and watching Brian with Joyce could end up being painful. And yet Lewis was very pleasant. She might have a nice time with him.

She met Brian's eyes. She couldn't read his expression.

"Okay," she said.

Joyce came up behind her, and agreed to the idea so readily that Grace's suspicions were confirmed. Joyce really liked Brian.

Ordering drinks, they sat around a table listening to the guitarist, who strummed nearby. They talked about music, and at one point, Lewis and Brian began discussing skiing. Grace and Joyce started talking together.

The more they talked, the more convinced Grace became that Joyce was a really sweet person who would be good for Brian.

And she absolutely *hated* the idea.

"What about you two?" Brian asked them suddenly. "Do either of you ladies ski?"

"Yes," they both answered.

"I used to go with my father and brothers and sister," Grace said, "although I haven't gone skiing for several years."

"I go skiing several times each winter," Joyce said, "though I'm not very good."

Oh, no. She had that in common with Brian. Grace wanted to kick herself for agreeing to have a drink with them. Seeing Brian's friendly smile, she felt her fingers clench.

This was not good. She should be trying to enjoy herself

with Lewis, who was a nice person. Instead, she was watching Brian and Joyce like a jealous woman.

Lewis began to talk about his favorite ski places, and Joyce mentioned one in Pennsylvania she liked. Grace felt Brian's eyes on her, and met them.

There was an odd expression there, an expression she couldn't read.

"Where do you like to ski?" she asked him.

Brian began to describe his favorite places.

A few minutes later Joyce looked at her watch.

"I'd better get going," she said, and Grace heard the reluctance in her voice. "I get up early for school."

They all left a few minutes later. As she drove away, Grace saw Brian and Lewis, standing by Brian's Jeep, still talking.

She was conscious of an achy feeling in her heart.

Brian liked Joyce. Who wouldn't? She was sweet and pleasant. Just the kind of woman he needed.

As she pulled into her driveway, Grace found herself wishing that Brian had been able to take her home, like he had from the Cotillion.

And more than anything, she wished she was in his arms right now. That he was kissing her and she was fervently kissing him back, just as they had that night.

The thought of him kissing Joyce—kissing anyone else—was like a knife.

When she entered the house, Lincoln barked happily, jumping near her, and Socks, on the chair, stretched approvingly.

"How was your date?" asked Yadira, coming out of the kitchen wrapped in a thick red bathrobe.

"He was nice, the nicest one so far," Grace said. She should feel happy, but all she felt was a hollowness inside. "And Brian had a very nice date."

Saying that hurt. A lot. Grace swallowed. It really bothered her.

Yadira was studying her, an anxious look on her face.

"Are you okay?" she asked, placing her hand on Grace's shoulder in a gesture of comfort.

"Yes. I—" But as she stared at Yadira, and the lovely diamond she wore, something clicked in Grace's brain.

Grace knew, quite suddenly, why seeing Brian with Joyce upset her so much. Why she'd felt hurt and jealous.

For one crazy minute, she wanted to both laugh and cry.

It had happened. It had really happened to her.

"What is it?" Yadira asked.

"Oh . . ." Grace whispered. "I'm in love. I'm in love with Brian!"

Chapter Eight

Grace sat on her bed with Yadira, sipping the hot cocoa Yadira had made them both. She had just finished giving Yadira a full account of the evening's events.

"Part of me is glad I finally found somebody to love," Grace concluded, sipping. "But part of me is sad."

"Why?" Yadira asked. She'd listened without interrupting as Grace told her story.

"Because he doesn't love me. He's afraid to love," Grace said with a quaver in her voice.

"That's what you said before. But look, Grace, I saw him with you that night after the hospital's ball. The look on his face—I could swear he was mesmerized or something. He may not be in love with you—yet—but he certainly isn't indifferent."

"He—he always refers to me as Flower Child," Grace said. "Like he thinks of me as a kid."

"He's probably just teasing. He wasn't acting as if he thought you were a child on Saturday," Yadira said wisely.

Grace blushed, remembering Brian's kiss. "No . . . we kissed."

"I thought so." Yadira's smile looked just a shade smug. "You wait. I think the guy really cares for you."

Some of her tension eased, and Grace smiled at her friend. "You always make me feel better."

"And you do the same for me—and everyone else." Yadira gave her a sudden hug. "You watch," she continued. "I predict that guy's going to be head over heels in love with you. He's just overly cautious because of his parents, and his ex-fiancée."

Lincoln came over suddenly, sat near Grace and looked up soulfully.

"Oh, good boy." Grace leaned down to give him a big hug. "I know you love me. And I love you too." Lincoln wagged his tail, then barked.

"Okay, okay," Grace said. "Time for your last run. C'mon." She finished her cocoa. "Thanks, Yadira."

"Just wait, girlfriend," Yadira said, grinning.

But later, in bed, doubts returned and crept through Grace. Would Brian ever be willing to take a chance on love?

Brian sat in his office, staring at the papers he'd picked up from the local hardware store. He should be thinking of something clever to promote their upcoming Presidents' Day sales.

But all he could think about was Grace Norwood.

Yesterday evening's date had been the most difficult of the three. Even though he was with the nicest woman he'd dated during the promotion, it had been hard to watch Grace with Lewis.

Lewis had been exactly the kind of guy that Grace should go for. Intelligent, not bad looking, with a pleasant personality, Lewis would have impressed most women.

And that was the problem. Because Brian knew in his heart he didn't want Grace to like Lewis.

He didn't want her to like any of her dates.

It was ridiculous, he knew. It wasn't as if he was Grace's boyfriend. He was behaving like an overprotective brother, he told himself.

He just didn't think any of the guys she'd dated were good enough for Grace.

Even Lewis, with his doctorate and pleasant personality, might not be good enough. Grace was a beautiful woman, with a sparkling personality, and an essential goodness that shined right through her.

He had to admit that Lewis had been thoughtful enough to ask Brian if he thought a group drink would be okay.

And Brian had supported the idea.

Not because he was eager to spend more time with Joyce. Yeah, she was nice enough, but she certainly didn't create the same kind of reaction he always had when he was in Grace's company. A reaction comprised of a sort of humming awareness through his whole self.

No, he'd gone along with the idea so he could keep an eye on Lewis and Grace.

He had been positive no one suspected his motives. That was, until he and Lewis were in the parking lot after Grace and Joyce had departed.

He had asked Lewis in his most casual manner if he'd enjoyed himself. But actually, he was probing to see what the other man thought of Grace, and had braced himself for Lewis's enthusiastic response.

And Lewis was enthusiastic, talking about how interesting, and friendly, Grace was. But then he'd flung out another comment.

"I kind of got the impression that you're interested in her yourself," Lewis had stated.

Brian had been startled, but he quickly recovered. "Oh, we're friends," he said, trying to sound as casual as he had previously. "I care about what happens to Grace."

Lewis had looked at him, then shrugged. "I thought it was more than that."

Brian had shaken his head. But once he was back home, seated in his reclining chair while he watched the news, he couldn't deny the fact that he was interested in Grace.

Very interested.

Too interested.

It looked like he had developed a thing for Grace.

Now he stared at the papers laying on his desk. What was he going to do? He'd have to do something. If someone like Lewis, who hardly knew him, could pick up on the fact that he had a thing for Grace, who else could? People here at WQNJ? Grace herself?

And he didn't want that to happen. Because he knew full well that it had nowhere to go.

He had to stop this before Grace got the wrong idea.

He felt an unaccustomed dull ache somewhere around his middle.

He stood up, glancing at his watch. Almost 2:00. Grace was here by now. He wasn't sure what he had to do, but he had to do something.

He went to search for her. Passing Charles's office with its open door, he heard her lilting voice and looked inside.

Grace was standing by Charles's desk. She wore a short denim skirt and a cream-colored sweater.

She looked gorgeous.

Brian swallowed. "Hi," he greeted them. He steeled himself against the appealing picture she made, telling his heart to stop its rapid beating.

"Hi." Her voice was soft, her smile warm.

Had Grace dressed this way to drive him crazy? He suppressed the thought instantly. No, of course not. Why would Grace dress up for him? She might wear her artsy clothes 90 percent of the time she was on the job, but she did wear stylish clothes too. She couldn't be trying to impress him.

Was she trying to impress Lewis?

That thought needled him.

Lewis would be impressed. Any human male would. Grace was attractive and sexy and . . .

"How was your date last night?" Charles was asking.

"Fine," Brian replied shortly. Then he noticed Grace studying him.

"Actually, it was very nice," he continued, leaning against the door. "Joyce is a very nice lady. I liked her the best of the three. We had a good time."

"Really?" Charles sounded more surprised than Brian would have thought.

Grace was still looking at him. Did he imagine she looked disappointed?

She was wearing that sophisticated perfume again, the one she'd worn to the hospital ball, not her usual sweet fruity scent. This scent was more mysterious and sophisticated.

"I—" She cleared her throat, then continued. "I thought she was sweet."

"Yes," Brian said. Grace's face wore an indifferent expression. He wondered if it was real or an act.

But why should she be pretending indifference? Brian asked himself harshly. A good-looking, lively young woman like Grace Norwood had better things to do then be concerned with her coworker's social life.

"How was your date?" he asked.

"My date? Oh, fine." Now her voice was neutral. "Lewis is intelligent and a nice guy . . ." Her voice wound down.

"But?" Charles prodded.

"But, oh, I don't know." Grace was looking at their employer now. Her stiff posture alerted Brian to the fact that she was not as relaxed as she sounded. Of course, he thought. She knows how to keep her voice calm. But she wasn't feeling calm inside, he could almost swear it.

"There was no . . . spark," Grace finished. "He's a nice guy, definitely, but that's it. Period. There was just nothing special there."

Brian couldn't prevent the sudden gladness that raced through him. He had no right to feel glad. No right.

But he did!

He made himself sound neutral. "Sometimes it takes time," he said.

She was looking at him, and he wished he could read her mind. She appeared to be considering something.

"That's definitely true for some people," she finally said. "I don't think it's true for me." She turned to Charles. "Anyway, we're really glad the station's going to do a program on Big

Brothers and Big Sisters. Since so many people tune in to Around the Town, maybe we'll get some more volunteers."

"Glad to help," Charles said. His eyes left Grace and turned to Brian.

For just one instant, Brian had the feeling that Charles was seeing right through him.

"Let me know soon who your Valentine's date choice is," he said.

Grace was on a short break later when she passed a tall woman standing at the receptionist's desk, talking to Tina.

". . . here to see Brian Talbot," she was saying, shaking some snow off the sleeve of her navy wool coat.

Oh no, Grace thought, *not another one.*

She was an attractive brunette, and the smile she was giving Tina was friendly. The woman looked vaguely familiar, but Grace couldn't place her. She approached her, ready to help Tina brush off another eager listener who wanted a date.

"Is this about the Valentine's date?" She asked the question politely. This woman was not haughty like the blond.

But Tina was smiling back at the woman. "You must be Brian's sister. He said you were coming in."

Brian's sister! No wonder she looked familiar. Grace could see the resemblance. She had the same eyes and coloring as her brother.

"I'm sorry," Grace apologized quickly. "We've had so many women coming in begging for a date with Brian, and I just assumed you were one of them. I'm Grace Norwood, the late-afternoon DJ." She extended her hand.

"Oh, yes, I listen to your program all the time," the woman said graciously, shaking Grace's hand. "I'm Lois Talbot. I'm here to take my brother out to dinner." Her voice was pleasing and well-modulated, and Grace guessed she would be a good speaker.

"What a nice sister," Grace said, smiling.

"So have women really been begging for a date with my little brother?" Lois asked, her eyebrows arching.

"They sure have," said Tina. "And one of them won't give up. She keeps coming back."

"Must be that Talbot charm," Lois said, laughing.

"Or the good looks," Tina added.

"I think Brian could use a girlfriend," Grace said quietly. "He's so—skeptical—about love and relationships."

"He has good reason," Lois said quietly. She was focusing on Grace, and for a moment Grace had the feeling that Lois was studying her.

"I know," Grace replied, her voice dropping. She was sure Tina and the others knew nothing about Brian's ex-girlfriend. "Maybe the right woman will change his attitude."

Lois gave her a brilliant smile. "The right person can really make a change."

Sudden hope flooded over Grace, and she smiled at Lois. "I agree."

"Tell me a little more about this Valentine's date thing," Lois urged Grace. "Brian doesn't talk about it much."

Grace spoke about how Charles had gotten carried away with the idea after her remark on the radio. And then how Brian had taken one of her own comments to start the campaign for a date for her.

"Has Brian liked any of his dates?" Lois asked.

"Well, he didn't care for the first two. But the third—" Grace stopped. There was a sudden lump in her throat. She took a long breath, inhaling Lois's subtle, classy cologne.

"His third date was a really nice woman," she finished. It was difficult to admit it. She wondered if Lois recognized the angst in her voice.

"I thought I heard a familiar voice."

Grace swung around, and found Brian standing behind her. She hadn't heard him approach.

Lois moved past Grace and gave her brother a big hug. When she stepped back, Grace saw Brian smiling affectionately at his sister, looking totally relaxed.

"Hey, Little Brother," Lois said. "Where do you want to eat?"

Grace didn't want to get in the way. She hastily said, "It was nice to meet you!" to Lois.

"You too!" Lois replied brightly. Grace started toward the staff room. She heard Brian suggesting several restaurants.

As she turned the corner, she caught Lois looking after her, a thoughtful expression on her pretty face.

Well, at least Brian has a nice sister, Grace thought. *He does have somebody to love, even if it's family.*

She was glad for him. He needed his sister, although Grace suspected he wouldn't admit it.

When she returned to the microphone a few minutes later, she dedicated a song to them.

"And this one's for Brian and his sister Lois," she said, hoping they were listening. " 'We Are Family'."

She sat back, feeling satisfied.

She wanted Brian to be happy. And she guessed his sister meant a lot to him.

Maybe, she thought idly, some day she'd get a chance to sit and talk with Lois and find out if there was a way to Brian's heart . . .

"That was very sweet of Grace, to dedicate a song to us," said Lois as she picked up her menu.

"Yeah, she's a sweet kid." Brian studied his sister for a moment. Something was different about Lois. Usually calm, Lois was more animated than normal, he thought. Something was up.

Maybe she'd gotten a raise or won the lottery or something. But no, money didn't mean a whole lot to her. Something else must be going on.

"What's happening?" he asked abruptly. "You seem different. Kind of excited."

Lois smiled widely. "I was wondering if you'd notice anything. I have to give you credit, Bri, most men don't pay attention to things like that."

"You are my sister, I know you pretty well. So what is it?"

She hesitated, then said in a rush, "I met someone." She was positively beaming.

"You met someone?" Brian couldn't help the surprise in his voice. The last time they'd discussed love, it had been like a four-letter word.

Both of them had been disheartened for years. Between their parents' bad example of marriage; Brian's social-climbing ex-girlfriend; and the fact that years ago Lois had discovered that her boyfriend was cheating on her with one of her friends—well, they'd both had it. Love was not a goal in their lives.

"Yes," she said, nodding happily. "Craig is—well, he's wonderful."

Brian felt fear. He drank some water, hoping to douse it. The last thing he wanted was to see his sister hurt.

He asked cautiously, "How long have you known him?"

"Not long," she admitted. "I met him at my friend Connie's holiday party. Remember I asked you to go, but you were skiing that whole weekend? Craig had just moved into the condo next to Connie and Bill. We hit it off, and . . . well, we've been seeing each other constantly. And we just kept getting closer."

"You never told me," Brian said.

"Well, you know me. I was afraid to believe it would go anywhere, and I didn't want to say anything. Only Connie knew." Lois's eyes sparkled. "But even though I was scared, things just happened. And Craig understood I was scared, and he was patient. He's very special." Her voice softened, and the look of love glowing on her face was unlike anything Brian had seen there before.

A waitress approached, and they stopped to give their orders.

"So when do I meet this lucky man?" Brian continued when the waitress left.

"Next week? He wants to meet you too. He wants to marry me, Brian. And I finally said yes!"

Brian whistled. "That's awful fast!"

But Lois shook her head. "Fast? Not at our age. I'm thirty-two, after all, and Craig's thirty. We're old enough to know what we want. I couldn't believe it at first, of course, after all these years, but—I found love, Bri!"

Her happy face alleviated some of Brian's fears.

"Does it bother you that there's an age difference?" he asked, curious.

"Of course not. It's not like we're in high school. Or like there's twenty years' difference."

He thought about the five years' difference between himself and Grace.

"Once you're over twenty-two or so, a few years is nothing," Lois continued. "Who cares if I'm a little older? It's a big deal when you're a teenager, but not now. Age doesn't matter as much as other things."

As Lois spoke, Brian felt a curious sensation. It was as if something had sparked inside him. Sparked, and then began to grow. Like a fire on a cold winter night such as this.

It took a minute for him to recognize the feeling. It was hope—something he hadn't felt for a long time.

Hope for *himself* as well as Lois.

"Is he good to you?" he questioned, leaning toward his sister.

"Oh, he is! I've never met such a caring person."

"Tell me about him," Brian said.

As they started on their salads, Lois described Craig. He owned a computer consulting company. He was hardworking but knew how to enjoy himself. He'd grown up in Connecticut, part of a close, loving family who Lois had met recently.

"There are really some nice normal families out there," she said. "Craig's parents are so sweet, and I like his brother and sister too."

"I can't wait to meet him," Brian said.

Their dinners arrived, and as Brian chewed his steak, it tasted especially delicious. Watching Lois's happy face, hearing the lilting note in her voice, he was genuinely happy to see his sister so obviously joyful. Lois deserved happiness.

She was a wonderful person, and if Craig was good to her, than he was content.

"Now tell me about this Valentine's thing." Lois switched topics.

"There's not much to tell," Brian said. He shook more salt on his baked potato.

Lois asked him questions about the dates he'd had. She laughed at his descriptions of the self-centered Tara and bossy Joanna.

"And what about your last date?" she asked, picking up a forkful of fettucini.

"Joyce is a nice woman, but nothing special," Brian said. "There was no . . . spark." He heard the echo of Grace's words in his own.

"And you haven't been going out with anyone else?" Lois pressed.

"No. Why?" Brian asked, wondering what his sister was getting at.

"What about your coworker Grace?" she asked abruptly.

Brian felt his mouth fall open, and quickly shut it. He wondered briefly if his sister was psychic.

"What about her?" he said slowly.

She was smiling, her expression just a shade smug. "Ah-ha. I was right. There *is* something there."

"What makes you think that? Are you a mind reader—or trying to be one?" he challenged.

Lois shook her head, still smiling. "No. It's just—I saw the look on her face when she was talking to you. Kind of, I don't know, wistful. And caring. I think she likes you, Brian. A lot. And I noticed you were looking her over pretty thoroughly."

Brian gave an elaborate shrug. "She looked hot in that outfit."

"C'mon, Brian, there's more to it than that, isn't there?" Lois asked. "You forget I know you well. I am your big sister," she added, repeating his words.

He stared at her. It seemed there was no hiding things from

his sister. And why should he? She was one of the few people he felt comfortable confiding in.

"Okay," he said suddenly, "I give in. You're right, Lo. I can't get her off my mind lately. It's like—like she's woven a spell around me or something."

Lois gave a little laugh. "A spell, huh? Sounds like more than that to me. Maybe love?"

But Brian interrupted. "No, it's not that. Let's just say I'm intrigued by her. And yes, I like her too. She's a very nice person. But of course she's too young for me," he added quickly, seeing Lois's 'I knew it' look.

"How old is she?" Lois leaned forward and put her chin in her hands.

"Only twenty-four."

"My goodness, Brian, that's nothing. So she's five years younger? Like I said, age doesn't really matter. It's the feelings that count."

Brian shook his head. "It's not just her chronological age. It's her attitude. She's young and naive—Grace believes the whole world is a wonderful place. She was brought up in an idealistic family. Her father's Woody Norwood."

"So?" Her word challenged him.

"So . . . she believes in things I don't. Like everlasting love."

Lois regarded him thoughtfully. "You know, even a year ago I might have agreed with you," she said. "But now that I've met Craig . . . you know, Brian, if you give things a chance, if you give *yourself* a chance, you might find you can believe in love too."

He stared at her. "I can't believe you're saying this," he muttered. "You've changed, Lois."

"Craig changed me. Love changed me." She smiled at him, her eyes sparkling. "If you give yourself that chance, I think love could make a difference to you too."

"I don't believe it," he said.

But the odd thing was, his heart had begun to beat more rapidly, and it occurred to him that he wanted to believe it.

"You may not believe it now," Lois said. "But do me a favor, will you? Try it. Just try. Follow the feelings you have for Grace and see what happens."

"But, what if—" Brian stopped. He sounded like a scared teenager.

Lois seemed to know what he was getting at. "What if you get hurt? You'll live. You have before. But you'll be more hurt if you don't take this chance. If you walk away from something that could be wonderful for you." She reached over and clasped his hand. "Believe me, Brian, I know. I almost didn't let Craig get close to me. Than I thought, if it doesn't work, I haven't lost anything. But if I don't take the chance, I'll be just as lonely as before, plus I'll be wondering what I might have missed."

She sat back, smiling widely. "I can't tell you how glad I am that I took a chance on loving."

Brian stared at Lois. Could his sister be right?

Could there be a chance that he and Grace might be more than friends?

And did he dare follow these crazy feelings wherever they might lead?

The phone's ring pierced the quiet, startling Grace. She almost dropped her book.

It was after 9:00, and the house was still except for a slight snoring from Lincoln. Yadira and Rafael had gone to visit his parents, and Grace was curled up on the couch, reading. She and Yadira had decided to read a couple of the Harry Potter books so they could discuss them with their "little sisters" LaShone and Maritza. Yadira had gotten ahead the day they'd had a snowday from school. Grace was finding the book fascinating and was eager to catch up.

It was a nice, comfortable Friday night, and Grace had been happy to get her mind off of Brian and Valentine's Day.

She placed a bookmark in the *Harry Potter* book and then reached over to get the phone.

"Hello?" she asked.

"Hi, Grace. How are you?"

She was surprised to hear Brian's mellow, deep voice. She reacted instantly, her heart accelerating.

"Oh, hi!" She couldn't stop the warmth that poured through her voice. "I'm fine. How are you? How was dinner with your sister? She's very nice, by the way."

"She liked you, too. In fact, she wants to see you again."

Grace's heart stumbled. Was this call merely about Brian trying to get her together with his sister? For what reason?

She said, more cautiously now, "oh? Why?"

"Oh, just to get together. She said I should bring you over some time. But that's not why I called," he went on. "I called because I thought—well, maybe we could get together ourselves. We can talk about our chosen Valentine's date and plans. . . ."

"Oh." Now her heart was really drooping.

"And we can have a good time," he continued in a rush, and Grace had a peculiar feeling he'd had trouble getting that last part out. "You said the other night you know how to ski. How about going skiing with me tomorrow?"

Her heart leaped up, spinning and dancing.

"I'd love to," Grace said. "I have an outfit but I'll have to rent skis and boots."

"Okay. I was thinking of heading out early tomorrow. With all this fresh powder, the slopes are going to be crowded. How about if I pick you up at eight?"

It was early for her for a Saturday. But she didn't care!

"Sounds great," she said, hearing the enthusiasm that rang through her tone.

"Okay. Dress in warm layers. I'll see you in the morning."

"I'm looking forward to it. But I'm warning you, I haven't skied for a couple of years."

He laughed. "That's all right, I'll help you up if you fall."

"Okay! See you tomorrow."

Brian said good-bye. Grace hung up, grinning at the phone.

It wasn't exactly a date, she told herself. Brian had made it sound like just a friendly get together.

But it was *something.*

She'd have to be up early. Grace decided to get ready for bed.

She let Lincoln out, and after a few minutes, called him in and gave him a treat. Socks appeared out of nowhere and she got a treat for him too.

She knew Yadira would be around tomorrow, so she wrote her a note in case she left before her roommate woke up, asking her to let out Lincoln a few times during the day, and to give him a snack. She'd call her during the day and let her know when she'd be back.

Grace hummed as she got into her pajamas. She stopped and smiled at her reflection.

She was humming "Somebody to Love."

Grace climbed into bed, but she didn't fall asleep right away. Instead, she found herself thinking about Brian. And reliving the moments when he'd kissed her.

Right now, at this very moment, she felt happy.

And hopeful. Because maybe, just maybe, Brian was beginning to care for her too.

Grace's spirits were high and she made no attempt to hide them when Brian picked her up in the morning. For the first time, he appeared as carefree as she did. They talked about everything from skiing to music as they drove up to the ski resort. Grace asked Brian about his sister, and he described Lois, and how close they'd always been. He also told Grace the story of Lois's cheating boyfriend, and how, recently, she had found someone.

"That's wonderful," Grace said quietly. Lois's happiness must be having an effect on Brian. He obviously cared about his sister's welfare. "Love really can make a difference in someone's life."

He shot her a teasing glance. "So says the idealistic Flower Child."

"Idealistic, true," she answered back, giving him a grin. "But it sounds like I'm correct."

"Well, maybe. So far Lois is happy." But Brian said it cheerfully, and Grace's heart zoomed up. Brian sounded, for the first time, like he might believe in her philosophy.

Once they arrived at the ski resort, they were busy renting equipment for Grace. Despite the crowd already there, there were lots of people working, so their wait was short.

Gliding up the mountain beside Brian on the lift, Grace felt a deep inner joy. She was here, with the man she loved. They were doing something fun together. What could be better?

It was obvious from the start that Brian was an excellent skier, while it took Grace a while to get back into the rhythm of skiing. Brian was patient, skiing easily next to her and giving her pointers the first two times they went down the slopes. By their third run, Grace was becoming reaccustomed to the motions and could relax and enjoy the feeling of flying over the snow.

"You're doing great," Brian said as they slid to the bottom together. "You're better than you led me to believe."

"Well, it's been several years since I went skiing," Grace said. "And I was never as good as you are."

"You're doing fine. Want to take the more challenging trail?" She must have looked skeptical, because he said, "We won't go on the most difficult slope."

"All right," she said bravely. "But if you want to go on the really difficult one, I'll watch."

"No," he said. "I can do that when I'm here alone. I want to spend time with you today."

Grace's heart flew higher than the ski lift.

They went down the more challenging slope twice. The second time, Grace fell. Brian skied over at once, checked to see that she was okay, and helped her to her feet. He followed her down the slope slowly, and when they got to the bottom, questioned her again.

"I'm okay, really," she told him. "It was just a little tumble. I was just out of breath." But it wasn't only her fall that caused that breathless feeling. It was the concern in Brian's face.

"I'm fine," she repeated. "Really!"

He cupped her face in his hands, his eyes searching her anxiously. The tingling that shot through her body had nothing to do with falling. Despite the sharp, cold air, Grace felt as warm as a fire on a cold winter night.

He cares! He cares! every fiber of her body was singing.

She smiled up at him.

Brian gave her a hard, swift kiss. His lips were warm and possessive. Thrills swept through Grace.

" 'C'mon," he said, his voice husky. "Let's take a break and get some lunch."

"Then I'll get back on the slopes," Grace told him.

"Okay, as long as you feel fine."

After they'd put their equipment in the lockers, they went into the large cafeteria. Brian kept his arm around her, and Grace enjoyed every minute of the protected feeling she had when she was tucked close beside him.

"Hey, Brian!" someone called from nearby.

A couple sitting at a nearby table waved to them. Brian introduced Grace to Nick and Colleen. He had met Nick several years ago while skiing here, he explained, and they'd gotten to know each other.

They ate lunch with them, and Grace enjoyed the camaraderie. Each moment she spent in Brian's company, she noticed every motion, every inflection of his voice. Being in love, she mused, made her senses more acute.

Brian appeared totally at ease, allowing her to get closer. She wasn't sure if it was because he was in the skiing element he loved, or because of his sister's happiness. Maybe both. The cynical side of him had faded, allowing his cheerful nature to shine through.

Maybe, she thought hopefully, it was partially because of her.

Once they finished lunch, they sat around for a few minutes, then went back to the slopes. They tried the medium trail twice, and Grace continued to improve with Brian's guidance.

"I'm really enjoying this!" she told him as they slid to a stop together.

"That's because you're getting better," Brian praised.

"And because of the company," she added, smiling up at him.

"The feeling's mutual." Once again he bent and gave her a quick kiss.

They went down the slope again, and Grace enjoyed the brisk air whooshing by, the feeling of being on top of the world with the man she loved. When they reached the bottom, Grace suggested Brian try the most difficult slope by himself. But he resisted again.

"I'll do it another time," he said.

The slopes were becoming more crowded, despite the fact that the day had turned cloudy and snowflakes began to drift down. As many snowboarders as skiers were on the slopes this afternoon, many of them teenagers. Grace had to be careful maneuvering around some of the more daring ones who rushed down the trail. The line at the lift lengthened, and by the time they went down again, snow was pelting them.

"Since you haven't skied for a long time, I don't want you to overdo it," Brian said. "Let's go down one more time, then pack it in."

"I'll probably be a little sore tomorrow," Grace admitted, "but that's okay, this has been fun!"

They skied down one last time, then separated to get changed. Grace grinned at her reflection in the locker room's mirror as she applied more lip balm. Her cheeks were rosy, and she knew it wasn't just from the fresh air and exercise.

She met up with Brian in the lobby. With a start she realized it was almost 4:00.

"I'll take your equipment back," Brian offered.

Grace took out her cell phone and called Yadira, who assured her she'd given Lincoln some treats and let him out several times.

"Rafael and I are going to see his friends down in Elizabeth. I won't be home till late," she said. "I'll give Lincoln dinner when I feed Socks."

"Thanks," Grace said, wondering if she should suggest treating Brian to dinner.

When Brian returned, he was smiling and still looked relaxed. Before she could say anything, he spoke.

"I know a great country restaurant where we can have dinner," he suggested. "It's not too far. I don't know about you, but I always work up an appetite when I'm skiing."

"That sounds great," Grace said.

The drive to the restaurant took them off the main highway onto a windy county road. They passed farmhouses and snow-covered fields, forests laden with thick snow, and a group of children building a snow fort.

The restaurant proved to be charming. An old country inn, it was paneled with dark wood, and candles glowed against the darkening evening. A large fireplace held a fire which burned brightly, the wood crackling and snapping. The delicious aroma of baked bread met Grace as a waitress led them to a table by a window.

She looked out, seeing the rolling hills of Sussex County. Several deer were treading across the snow-covered field in the back.

"This is beautiful," Grace said. "It has real country ambiance."

They ordered, then took salads from the salad bar.

When they returned to their table, there was homemade bread and a crock of fresh butter waiting for them, along with two glasses of wine.

As they ate they talked about the day's skiing. Grace expressed her admiration for Brian's skill.

"I've loved to ski since I was very young," he said. "I don't do anything extreme, but I love the sensation of moving over the snow and speeding down the mountain."

"I can see you're an expert," Grace said.

"Not exactly, but thanks. You're good, too, Grace."

"Thank you." Grace said the words demurely, but her heart was racing. She spread the creamy butter on her bread, then tasted it. The hearty bread was delicious.

Swallowing, she took a sip of the mellow wine. Brian was studying her, and she wondered what he was thinking.

"I bet you can't wait to go skiing again," she said lightly.

He shook his head. "That wasn't what I was thinking about. I mean, I want to go skiing again, but I was thinking about . . . you."

Something inside of Grace was glowing as much as the dark green candle on their table.

He smiled. "I was just thinking that Jonathan, Fred, and Lewis would all be fighting me for a chance to have dinner with you tonight."

"Well, I wouldn't want to be here with them. I prefer being here with you." She smiled and took another sip of wine. "I'm sure Tara, Joanna, and Joyce would be outrageously jealous if they knew I was with you."

As she placed the wine goblet back down, it clicked against the table.

Brian leaned forward, capturing her hand in both of his. His hands were warm, the skin slightly rough against her smoother skin. He squeezed her hand.

"They can be jealous all they want. I'd rather be here with you any day."

Her heart was beating somewhere up near her throat.

She placed her other hand on his, and for a moment they simply stared at each other. Grace lost herself in Brian's golden-brown gaze. His eyes were bright, and the expression there melted her insides.

He lifted her hands and kissed them tenderly.

The kiss sent a bolt of electricity shooting through her nervous system.

For a moment time stopped. Then the clatter of dishes from nearby penetrated their reverie. Brian released her hands, and sat back.

Their dinners were ready. As the waitress served them, Grace smiled softly at Brian. This was turning into one of the best evenings of her life, and she wondered if he had any idea how much he meant to her.

The meal was delicious. As they ate, Grace flirted subtly with Brian, offering him a bite of her chicken, touching his hand when they both reached for their wineglasses. Brian's eyes gleamed, and he responded in kind.

They ordered homemade apple pie for dessert. When it arrived, Brian teased her, asking her if all Flower Children were this beautiful.

"Beautiful on the inside and outside," Grace said. "I know my parents and lots of their friends from that era are that way." She took a small forkful of the pie. The sweet apple filling was warm and spiked with cinnamon.

"Your mother must have looked a lot like you when she was younger. But no one is quite like you, Grace. You are gorgeous, inside and out." He put his fork down, saying the words solemnly.

Grace's whole body was vibrating with happiness. "Thank you," she said. "Did I ever tell you that I think you're handsome and the most masculine-looking man I know?"

Brian looked very pleased. "Thank you," he said. "It sounds like we're a mutual admiration society."

Grace laughed. "Maybe I'll start the Friends of Brian Talbot Society."

"Only if we can have a Grace Norwood Fan Club," he answered back, laughing.

They left shortly afterward. Snowflakes continued to drift down at intervals as they drove south along the Sussex County roads. The snow-covered hills glowed in the moonlight. They listened to WQNJ, talking occasionally, enveloped in comfortable silence the rest of the time.

Their dinner was even more wonderful than the evening they'd spent together at the hospital's ball, Grace thought. Because not only were they by themselves, but Brian had lost his skepticism, and in its place was a tenderness that she found thrilling.

It took a little over an hour before they pulled into the driveway of the house Grace shared with Yadira.

"Come in, and I'll make us some hot cocoa." Grace invited.

"That sounds good," Brian said. "How are you? Are you sore?"

"Only a tiny bit," Grace admitted. "But it was worth it! I had a wonderful day."

They entered the house, and Lincoln greeted Brian like an old friend before Grace let him outside for a run. She heated up hot water, brought Lincoln in and gave him and Socks treats. She brought the WQNJ mugs into the living room, where Brian sat on the couch.

He'd turned on the CD player and selected one of her favorite Beatles CDs. Grace handed him a mug and curled up beside him on the couch, kicking off her shoes.

"Your dog is great," Brian said, scratching Lincoln behind the ears. Lincoln's tail waved back and forth as he gave Brian his doggy smile.

"Did you ever have a dog?" Grace asked.

"We had a husky, Chief, when I was younger. I like big dogs."

"We always had dogs and cats," Grace said, sipping her cocoa.

Brian tasted the cocoa. "This is good—perfect for a winter night."

They sat listening to the Beatles' "Abbey Road" album. After a few minutes, Brian reached over and plucked Grace's mug from her.

"You know what else is perfect for a winter night?" he asked, setting the mug down on the coffee table beside his.

"What?" Grace asked archly, although she suspected she knew the answer.

"Getting close." Brian smiled, and pulled her into his arms.

Grace went willingly. The faint scent of Brian's masculine aftershave reached her just before his lips captured hers. Her hands instinctively wound around his neck, and Brian tightened his hold on her.

Nothing had ever made her feel the way she did when Brian kissed her. It was as if she was a musical note, floating through the air, spinning and gliding.

Her fingers stroked Brian's neck, touching the springy hair there, feeling the warmth of his skin.

His lips left hers momentarily. "Grace . . . Grace . . ." he murmured, kissing her throat, her cheek, her ear. Then they returned to hers again, as if he couldn't keep away.

Grace made a throaty little noise. Brian's kiss became harder, more demanding.

Every part of Grace was sizzling, electrified by Brian's kiss.

She loved him. She loved him.

The words bubbled in her soul, and trembled on her lips.

Brian released her lips and took a long breath.

The words tumbled out of her mouth.

"I love you," she whispered.

Grace felt Brian start.

Oh no, what had she done?

She had never been the kind to hide her feelings. She knew she felt love. But she also knew Brian wasn't ready to hear those words.

For a moment, Grace was sorry she'd said it.

And then, she was flooded with another feeling. Gladness. She was glad she'd finally said the words. She was proud of this feeling. And she wanted Brian to know that.

She pulled back slightly, and Brian's fingers loosened their tight grip.

She looked at him.

Brian's cheeks were flushed, and he sucked in his breath audibly. His eyes met hers. She recognized confusion there.

"I love you," she repeated, placing her hand gently against his cheek. This time her voice rang clear and strong. No matter what, she was glad to experience this emotion, to finally know this earthshaking feeling.

"Grace . . ." Brian's hand trembled as he smoothed back her hair. His fingers slid to her chin, and he cupped it, searching her face.

For a moment, he was stunned.

She loved him. Grace loved him.

And then a gigantic wave of happiness tumbled through him and he swallowed, overcome. He hugged her close.

After a few moments he drew back, meeting Grace's adoring look. Slowly, a chill crept up his spine.

Love. He'd sworn he'd never give in to that emotion again. It took too much from you.

But looking at Grace, he wondered how on earth he could stop himself from caring for her.

He already cared, too much. He was afraid—afraid he loved her too.

"Grace—" He stopped. He saw a questioning look cloud her eyes.

"This love thing—I don't know." Suddenly, unable to bear seeing any pain in her face, he pulled her tightly against him, burying his face in her soft chocolate hair. "I just don't know."

"That's all right." Her voice was sure and strong, without a hint of uncertainty. "I understand, Brian, believe me. I know what you've been through. It's okay if you're not sure."

He pulled back slightly so he could gaze at her again. "Grace . . . I don't want to hurt you, but I don't know. I don't know how I feel. Just—give me some time, okay?"

Her brilliant smile lit her face. Lit the whole room, the whole universe.

"Okay," she said.

He gathered her into his arms again.

The following day passed swiftly. From the moment she awoke, Grace felt like she was surrounded by bright music.

Brian called and they went to the movies with Yadira and Rafael. Then they called Will and Crystal, and invited them to join the four at the Australian Steak House. They all talked and laughed. Grace had a wonderful time, and the fact that Brian was constantly squeezing her hand, winking at her, or leaning over for a quick kiss gave the whole day a rosy glow.

When Grace went to the ladies' room, Crystal and Yadira followed.

"You look like a couple in love," Yadira said with a smile.

Grace nodded. There was no pretending otherwise.

Crystal, too, was smiling.

"I knew there was something cooking between you and Brian," she said.

When they returned to the table, Brian's adoring look made Grace's insides melt faster than snow possibly could.

When Brian said good-bye that night, his kiss was long and lingering. And Grace felt the tremors down to her toes.

"Good night, sweetheart," he whispered, stroking her hair.

"Good night," she whispered, standing on tiptoe to give him one more kiss. "Sweet dreams."

"I'll dream of you." His smile was toasty warm.

She gazed out after him as he walked to his car, waved, and got in.

Sweetheart. He'd called her sweetheart!

When Grace went to sleep, she was unbelievably happy.

Just before she fell asleep, it occurred to her that she and Brian had never discussed their Valentine's dates.

Monday dawned sunny but very cold. Grace woke feeling as bright as the sky. She couldn't wait to get into the radio station to see Brian again.

Discussing their Valentine's dates was at the top of her agenda. February 14th was at the end of the week, and they had to finalize their plans now.

Over breakfast, she thought about the Valentine's date promotion. The idea had been to find a date—or perhaps a special someone—for Brian, and for her.

And they had found each other.

Grace smiled. Who would have guessed this would happen?

Maybe, she mused, Charles Armstrong had suspected all along. He always seemed to watch Brian and her with a keen interest. Maybe he had even thought that in some convoluted way, this promotion would have the opposite effect of bringing them closer.

Whatever had been in his mind, Grace could view it with amusement now. Because she knew in her heart that Brian cared, and although he hadn't voiced it yet, she believed he, too, was falling in love.

So, what to do about the big Valentine's date?

She considered the problem as she washed off her dishes.

The restaurant was reserved, flowers and champagne had been ordered, and two limousines were booked for the evening for Grace, Brian and their dates.

It was a shame, really, that they couldn't get Lewis together with Joyce while she paired off with Brian.

Grace went still.

Well, why not?

Why not send Joyce and Lewis out on a date together?

Her heart hammering, Grace turned to Lincoln, who lay contentedly dozing in a corner.

"I just had a brilliant idea!" she announced.

Wag, wag, wag, his tail thumped. He yawned, stretched, and promptly went back to sleep.

He obviously wasn't too impressed. But Grace was excited.

They could get Lewis together with Joyce and send them on the ultimate dream date!

Quickly, she scribbled her idea on a pad, ripped off the paper, and put it with her things to bring into work. If Brian was out on appointments, she could leave the suggestion on his desk.

She hummed while she finished getting ready to go into the station.

When Grace arrived at WQNJ, Tina informed her that Brian was out on several appointments and she wasn't sure when he'd return. In case she was on the air when he did, Grace dropped the note about Joyce and Lewis on his desk, then went to her own.

Will was on the radio, announcing an upcoming song by the Temptations. "It makes me think about my own girlfriend," he said jovially. "Hey, Crystal, I know you usually listen to WQNJ on your lunch break. If you're listening, this one's for you. I love you."

How sweet! Grace's eyes misted over as the first notes of "My Girl" began. Will was head over heels in love with her sister, and wanted the whole world to know. She was so happy for them both. She hoped Crystal was listening.

She found a folder on her desk, and quickly began to go through the script for a St. Patrick's Day ad for a local pub. Brian had written another amusing commercial, and she was experimenting with different leprechaun voices when her phone buzzed.

"Grace?" It was Tina. "Could you come out to the lobby? I have a bit of a problem, and Brian and Charles aren't here."

"Sure." She hung up. Wondering what the problem could be, Grace stood up and went out to the reception area.

She found Tina standing by her desk, facing the tall blond who'd been in twice before.

Tina's face was flushed, and Grace could tell by her stance that the older woman was angry.

And so was the blond. Her lovely features held a scornful expression, marring her good looks. She had taken off her elegant coat and her hands were placed on her hips in a defiant pose.

"I'm not leaving until I see Brian Talbot," the blond declared, her voice haughty. Her strong perfume bombarded Grace.

Grace guessed that the woman and Tina must have had words already. Tina could usually handle things herself. The blond must have done something to make Tina call for reinforcements.

"Brian is not here," Grace said, slowly and carefully, as if speaking to a much younger child. "So you can't see him."

The blond whirled around and looked at Grace, her glance taking in Grace's jeans and simple dark red sweater.

"She didn't believe me when I told her that," Tina said darkly.

"You can leave him a note," Grace said. A cold, uneasy feeling was welling up inside of her, like frost creeping across the ground on a cold winter night. She tried to shake it off.

"Well, I'm going to see for myself. I bet he is here," the woman said, and marched off down the corridor.

Tina and Grace looked at each other. "Should I call the police?" Tina asked hopefully.

"I don't think Charles would like that. We'll try to handle it ourselves," Grace said. "If necessary, I'll get Will if she simply won't leave. We'll call the police as a last resort."

She hurried after the woman.

The woman was cruising down the hall, peeking into offices.

"Just a minute!" Grace said in her most commanding voice. "You can't interrupt people while they're working."

"Then tell me where he is!" the blond spat out. "I demand to see him. He's going to be mad when he finds out you and the receptionist wouldn't let me see him! I know he'll want to date me!" Her voice rose to a near shriek.

"He's already had his three dates." Grace said. Could this woman be some kind of crazed fan who'd fallen for Brian after she'd heard his voice on the radio? News stories about stalkers flashed through her mind. Stalkers didn't have to be men. Women could stalk their victims, carrying weapons.

Maybe they *should* call the police.

The woman stopped at the door labeled *Brian Talbot*. Without a knock she flung the door wide, and stepped inside.

And stopped.

"I told you he wasn't here," Grace said. She didn't try to hide the smugness in her voice.

The blond turned back, scowling.

"I don't believe anything you say," she snapped. She strode back up the hall toward the reception area.

Grace followed quickly. For some reason, the cold feeling in her stomach was getting worse.

"I guess I have to wait," the blond announced as she approached the lobby.

Grace was glad to see that Jan had joined Tina. She must have heard the commotion, or Tina had called her too.

"Page Brian and tell him he has company," the woman ordered.

"I will not," Tina said defiantly.

Grace wanted to handle this herself, but she wondered if having Brian return and tell the blond he wasn't going to date her might not be the best thing.

"Well, you can wait," she told the woman in her most frigid voice. "But it might be a long wait. I have no idea when he'll be back."

"But Mr. Armstrong, the station's manager, will be back here any minute," Jan added.

As if on cue, Grace saw through the window that two Jeeps were pulling into the parking lot, one right after the other.

She didn't say anything, but Tina noticed too, and blurted out, "Here comes our manager and Brian. You can say what you want to them!" The look on Tina's face was one of anticipation.

Grace was curious as to what Brian's reaction would be to the obnoxious woman. It could be interesting. So why didn't she feel better? Why did she have this anxious feeling?

She waited, as the woman stood, watching the door.

There was laughter outside, and then the door opened. Charles Armstrong entered, chuckling, and Brian strode in right behind him.

Seeing the group in front of them, they both fell silent.

"Brian!" the woman screeched, and launched herself at him.

In the split second before she reached Brian, Grace knew.

It was *her.*

Shock registered on Brian's face. He braced himself just before the blond landed against him, grasping for his shoulders.

"Victoria!"

Chapter Nine

Victoria—the woman who'd broken Brian's heart! She should have guessed who the blond was. Grace stiffened as she heard someone behind her gasp.

"Oh, Brian, I've missed you so much," Victoria was saying.

Brian stepped back, untangling the arms clinging to his neck. His eyes met Grace's and she recognized that he was stunned.

But he was recovering quickly, and Grace observed his face going from stark white to red.

"You know this woman?" Tina's tone was scathing.

"Of *course* he knows me," Victoria shot back, not even looking at Tina.

"What are you doing here?" Brian demanded, pushing Victoria's arms away.

"I came to see you, of course. I knew as soon as you saw me you'd want me to be your Valentine's date," Victoria said softly, her voice now gently chiding. She moved her arms toward Brian.

Grace struggled to maintain a composed expression as she watched the two. She felt stifled by Victoria's heavy perfume, almost sickened by it.

"The last time I saw you, you were engaged." Brian's voice was clipped, and Grace's fingers tensed. He stepped back.

Grace knew his shock was subsiding, and was being replaced by something else. "And I read you'd gotten married."

"The biggest mistake of my life," Victoria said, drooping visibly. Her eyes welled up.

What an act! Grace thought. *She doesn't care about Brian. She only cares for herself!*

"I knew soon after I married him it was a mistake," Victoria said sadly, wiping at her eyes. "I should have stayed with you. I was—a little crazy, I guess, and immature. I gave up the best thing that ever happened to me." She looked up at Brian beseechingly and reached out towards him.

"Oh, *puh-lease.*" Tina's voice, coming from next to Grace, was low but audible.

Victoria shot her a look that would have killed a weaker woman. But Tina stood her ground.

Whether Brian heard Tina's scoffing comment or not was uncertain, since he showed no reaction. He stepped back further, and his face had become hard, unyielding.

"You expect me to believe you?" His voice was like granite, and Grace almost flinched.

"Yes! Please!" Victoria looked up at him with an entreating expression. "It's the truth. I made a terrible mistake. And now I want to put it right," she finished, swiping at another invisible tear.

Grace was still cold, but she was feeling disgust, too. Did Victoria really believe she could step back into Brian's life just like that?

Oh, no, Grace thought, *what if Brian likes the idea?*

But as Grace focused on Brian's face, it was apparent he didn't like the idea. He was angry. Very angry.

Her relief only lasted a few seconds.

Brian's anger boiled over, and his voice was cold when he spoke. "You chose your path, Victoria. Money and status. Now go find some other fool who'll believe that you care for him instead of his money."

Someone—Tina or Jan—gasped again.

Something about his voice, his expression, made Grace

shiver. He wasn't just angry. He was—she wasn't certain what he was. But he was more than just angry.

Victoria's face had gone chalk-white. "You can't mean that," she said, and Grace realized Victoria had forgotten about the others in the room and had quit acting. "It's me, Brian, I'm back. Your love."

"You're not my love," Brian snapped.

Grace held her breath, waiting for him to say something, to look at her, to make some gesture. Nothing happened. His eyes were still glued to Victoria, who had started to shake.

I'm your love, Grace wanted to whisper. She clamped her lips together, feeling a tightening in her stomach.

Victoria had taken a step toward Brian. "Brian! Please! You've got to give me another chance!"

"You had your chance. You blew it," he said, his voice colder than the icicles hanging from the station's roof. "I have nothing more to say."

"Brian! Brian, I—"

Brian turned and marched off down the corridor without another word.

Grace had to stop herself from dashing after Brian. Her knees felt weak as she regarded Brian's stiff back. Turning to look at Victoria, she saw the woman was staggering to a chair. Reaching it, she slumped into it. Her face was a mask of disbelief.

Did Victoria just assume Brian would welcome her back with open arms? Grace wondered. From Victoria's sagging posture, it seemed that's exactly what she had expected.

For the first time, Charles spoke.

"I think you've done enough damage," he said, in a voice Grace had never heard him use before. Her good-natured employer was staring at Victoria with contempt.

Victoria raised her eyes to look at Charles. And as Grace watched, Victoria's expression went from surprise to fear.

"Now please leave," Charles ordered.

Victoria got up, and Grace saw her hands were trembling. Without another word she picked up her coat, swung it around her shoulders, and walked out the door. Grace caught a glimpse of real tears in her eyes.

It seemed that Victoria had gotten the same treatment she'd given Brian years ago.

"Good riddance." Tina's voice sounded smug as the door shut behind Victoria.

"What a witch," Jan said.

"Yes," Charles said. His face still reflected anger—and disdain. "That woman has a lot of nerve, to think she could just waltz back into Brian's life, and disrupt things around here." He turned and regarded Grace.

And in that moment Grace knew that her employer was aware of what was going on between herself and Brian.

Maybe her suspicion was correct, and he'd even helped engineer it.

She swallowed. Tina and Jan were looking at her too, curiosity plainly written on their faces.

"I'm glad he told her off." Grace's voice was scratchy. "And you too, Charles."

"We weren't sure what to do," Tina said. "I was thinking of calling the police when she wouldn't leave."

"If she shows up again, do that," Charles told them. "However, I have a feeling that Miss High and Mighty won't show her face here again."

"I have a feeling you're right," Tina concurred, smiling.

Still cold, Grace wished she could follow Brian. But she knew he'd need a cooling off period. She restrained herself.

"Are you all right?" Charles's voice was gentle now, as he continued to look at Grace.

"I—yes." Grace swallowed. "That's the woman who kept coming to see Brian, Charles. I had no idea that she—that she was Brian's old girlfriend." That she was the one who broke his heart, she added silently.

The knot in her stomach remained tightly coiled.

Oh, no, her mind kept repeating. *Oh no.* Of all times to be reminded of the woman who broke his heart—why did Victoria have to show up *now?* Now, when it seemed that Brian was finally beginning to trust her and believe in love?

Would Victoria's presence today adversely affect their relationship?

Grace was afraid it would. Judging by his extreme reaction, Victoria's behavior had reminded Brian of all the hurt he'd experienced in the past.

Tina cleared her throat. Grace started, snapping back to the present. Charles, Tina, and Jan were all staring at her.

"I'll see if I can calm Brian down," she said tonelessly.

Charles put out a hand. "Maybe you'd better wait a few minutes."

Grace nodded. "Okay. I'll be in my office."

She escaped to the quiet haven of her office, closing the door but not completely. She wanted to hear if Brian came out of his office.

Sinking into her chair, Grace leaned her head on her hands.

Victoria could not have appeared at a worse time, she thought glumly. Just as Brian had begun to trust her, and his feelings—Victoria had showed up.

And smashed those hopes just as completely as a discordant note shattering glass.

Would Brian trust his feelings after this?

Grace bit her lip. She loved Brian, but she was afraid, terribly afraid, that the love he'd started to experience for her would die as surely as if Victoria had killed it.

She stood up, and began pacing. What could she do? She knew Brian needed to cool off a bit, get a grip on his emotions and the events of the afternoon, get some distance and perspective. She was dying to rush into his office and try to talk to him, but she knew he needed time by himself.

But not too much time, she decided. Too much time could cause him to brood.

She stopped pacing. No, she didn't want him to sit there, concentrating on Victoria and her treachery, for too long. She wanted to remind him there were other kinds of people in the world.

Grace glanced at her watch. Scarcely ten minutes had gone by since Brian had stalked away from Victoria. She'd wait another ten, then go in and see him.

She tried to resume going over the St. Patrick's Day commercial, but it was impossible to concentrate. She heard Jan in the hall, talking to Charles about the local Habitat for Humanity and their newest project. She listened half-heartedly to the Creedence Clearwater Revival song that Will had just introduced.

Down the hall, a phone rang.

Everything seemed normal on the outside.

But it wasn't. Grace felt as if a dark cloud was hanging over her, and she knew it must be worse for Brian.

She got up to gaze out the window. Wind blew gusts of snow across the field adjacent to the station. The day had grown more gray, the sunlight slowly fading, and now the darker clouds skidding across the sky seemed to match her mood.

She turned abruptly to look at the digital clock. Another minute, and she'd go see Brian.

The minute seemed to take an hour.

She looked outside again, then at the papers on her desk. Then at her pictures of Lincoln, her siblings and her parents. Taking a deep breath, she tried to relax her taut muscles.

When the last number on the clock moved from six to seven, she left the office and walked down the hall to Brian's, trying not to hurry.

She rapped softly on the door.

"Yes?" She could hear the sharp edge in Brian's voice.

"It's me, Grace. May I come in?" Her heart was thudding. "Okay."

Grace entered, closing the door behind her, and turned to face Brian.

He was sitting at his desk, a stack of papers between his hands, but the dazed look on his face told her clearly he wasn't concentrating on work.

Grace took the seat in front of him. "I want to talk to you

about that woman," she said, keeping her voice even and well-modulated. "Victoria."

"There's nothing to say." It came out sharply.

Grace had to stop herself from flinching at his tone.

"I think there is. It's obviously—" She searched for a word that was softer than what she really meant. "—disturbed you." Shaken, even shocked him, was more like it. But she knew men didn't like to admit that sort of thing.

"I'm fine."

"Are you?" Again, she kept her voice soft. "Brian, I know you weren't happy about seeing her. It probably brought back some bad memories."

"You can say that again," he said, his tone dark. He focused on Grace's face, and she was glad to see the look in his eyes soften. "Grace, I—" He stopped, shook his head. When he spoke again, his voice wasn't as angry, but more resigned.

"Victoria reminded me about all the reasons I had for not falling in love again."

Pain stabbed her soul.

"I understand," she said softly. "But please remember, not all women are like Victoria." As Brian's eyes met hers, she took a shallow breath. His expression was haunted, and the ache inside her grew. She clenched her hands, scraping the stiff fabric of her jeans.

Brian didn't reply.

"I'm not like Victoria," she continued, her voice falling to a whisper.

Brian stared at her, and Grace wished desperately she could read his thoughts.

She waited, and finally, he spoke.

"I know you're a much kinder person than Victoria," he said slowly. "And I know you're not interested in money and status. But . . ."

Grace prompted, "But . . . ?"

"But I'm afraid I just can't believe in love. Not lasting love."

This time, Grace couldn't stop herself from flinching. The ache inside had turned to a block of ice.

"Brian—" Her voice was hoarse.

"I'm sorry, Grace." Brian's mouth set in a grim line. His voice grew stronger, more determined as he spoke. "I just can't give you any hope that I'll feel differently in a day or a week or a month. I told you before, I didn't trust this love thing."

Grace swallowed. "I know you did. You were always honest. But give it some time. Give me a chance to prove that not everyone is a Victoria."

The look he sent her was a mix of pain and fear. "I don't know. I just don't know anymore. What you feel for me may just be idealistic hope."

Even as her insides ached, Grace felt an additional ache for Brian's own pain. All his terrible memories had resurfaced, and Grace thought grimly that she could have cheerfully dropped Victoria on a deserted island in the middle of the ocean. The Arctic Ocean.

She reached out gingerly to take Brian's hand.

He jerked back.

It was like a slap. Grace gasped.

"I'm sorry, Grace." Brian's voice was hoarse, his expression even more haunted as he gazed at her. "I just can't fall in love."

"You mean you won't allow yourself too." Grace's own voice was hushed. Her heart was sinking down to her toes.

"I guess you're right. I just can't—won't—allow myself to get so involved again. I can't risk it. Do you understand?" His voice had taken on a desperate note. "Not after—all I went through. I think we need to cool our relationship off."

She tried one more argument. "But that was a long time ago. And you said yourself I'm not like Victoria."

Oh no, she thought, *I sound like I'm pleading.*

Surely she had more backbone than that. Grace stiffened her spine, meeting Brian's confused look.

"Never mind," she said suddenly. "If that's what you want,

fine. You know I love you, Brian, but I'm not going to beg for your love." She gripped the edge of his desk, leaning toward him, a spurt of anger going through her. Couldn't he see that she was *nothing* like Victoria? That she would never hurt him like Victoria had?

Before he could say another word, she continued, her voice rising with her own hurt and frustration. "Maybe when you've had time to think, you'll finally realize that I'm a different woman than Victoria."

Grace stood up abruptly and left the room.

She fought tears as she closed the door behind her.

Before she returned to her office, she went to the room where the CDs were stored. With determination, she searched for "Evil Ways" and "Evil Woman."

Brian's hands reached out instinctively, and he stood and started forward, then stopped.

The total confusion he'd been feeling for the last few minutes swirled inside him, through his middle, leaping into his mind. He shook his head, wishing he could think straight.

Victoria's appearance had brought back memories he had buried long ago. Memories of her callousness and treachery, and how she'd hurt him. Memories that had been hidden but were still there, waiting for this opportunity to bombard him.

On the radio, he heard Will introducing a song. The tune flowed past him, and he registered words about everlasting love.

Love—ha! he thought grimly. True love was something that didn't exist. At least not for him.

He knew he could never depend on love. Even with Grace, the sweetest, most caring person he'd ever met.

Or at least, he thought she was the most caring.

But he'd thought Victoria loved him. And he'd been wrong about her.

He could be wrong about Grace, too.

Because you could be deceived. Just when you thought you

had found your true love, a woman could turn around and laugh in your face.

He gritted his teeth, the unpleasant tenseness surging through him.

He knew he wasn't the only one hurting. Victoria—well, he doubted she had a sincere bone in her body. That had been a clever act.

For some reason, Victoria wanted him back in her life. Maybe, he thought, she had no one else. Maybe all the men she knew had wised up to her true character.

But Grace hadn't been acting. She was genuinely hurt, because he'd made it plain that he wanted to step away from their relationship.

It was better this way, he told himself. Better for them both. Grace was obviously wounded, and angry too. But that was better than continuing their relationship and having her more hurt later on when he broke it off.

Because he couldn't continue this way. He was too close to loving her, too perilously close. And he couldn't allow that to happen.

Brian began pacing back and forth in his office.

It was terrible that he had already allowed Grace to fall in love with him. He should have stopped their relationship early on. He should have realized that she was the type to fall quickly in love, like her parents.

His pacing had become almost frenzied. He stopped. The normally cozy office appeared to have shrunk, and the walls seemed to be closing in on him. It was warm inside, too warm.

He couldn't remain here, visualizing Grace's strained expression, hearing the echoes of pain in her voice.

He grabbed his coat, his briefcase, and bolted out the door.

Grace was not quite sure how she made it through the rest of the afternoon and early evening. Her hurt and anger gradually chilled, turning into a frozen numbness. She went through the rote motions of her job, talked on the air, and if she wasn't quite as happy-go-lucky as she usually was, well, everyone was entitled to an off day, weren't they?

She got some pleasure from playing "Evil Ways" and "Evil Woman." She introduced them with the simple comment that here were two songs about evil women. She was sure her coworkers would know why she was playing them. She wished she had remembered to look for "Witchy Woman" too.

What, she wondered, would Brian think?

She didn't know. She only knew that playing those songs made her feel a little better.

But when she signed off, she took a long, shaky breath.

She dragged herself home, relieved to be able to stop the cheerful act. She wasn't cheerful. She was far from it. She felt weary and worn.

Lincoln's enthusiastic greeting soothed her raw nerves, and she hugged the dog, who licked her face. Grabbing his leash, she took him for a long walk.

The winter air felt refreshing against her warm cheeks. It was good to move around, to be herself, with no one to perform for.

When they entered the house, Yadira sat waiting, already in pajamas, with a mug of hot cocoa.

"Here," she said, handing it to Grace as Grace shrugged out of her coat.

"Thanks," Grace said. She hung the coat on a peg and got Lincoln a treat. Sliding off her boots, she went to sit on the couch where Yadira was already perched, a content Socks half-asleep on her lap.

"How did you know I needed this?" Grace asked, sipping the hot liquid.

"Something in your voice when you were talking to Lincoln. So what's going on?"

Grace settled into a corner of the couch. "Something awful happened today."

"Tell me." Yadira sat back, her eyes fastened on Grace.

Grace's voice wobbled as she told her best friend about Victoria's arrival, Brian's reaction, and the scene between

Brian and herself. She stopped fighting the tears and let them slide down her cheek.

"I'm afraid it's . . . over between Brian and me," she choked out.

Yadira pulled a tissue from the pocket of her robe and handed it to Grace. Then she slipped a comforting hand on her shoulder as Grace blew her nose loudly.

"Why?" she asked softly. "Just because he's upset right now? That could be nothing. Less than nothing. It's probably just a temporary feeling on his part, because she brought out all his old memories of being hurt. Once he sits down and really thinks about it, he should see—if he's the kind of person I think he is—that that was a long time ago and a different woman. He may just need some time to put it in perspective." Yadira's voice was reassuring.

Grace smiled at her friend, knowing it must look weak. "It's sweet of you to say so, but, I doubt it. You should have seen his face and heard his voice, Yadira. I'm positive he means what he says. He doesn't believe in love."

"He means it now, but in another few days, he could think differently."

"I hope so. I really hope so," Grace murmured.

Yadira reached out and hugged her. Socks, disturbed from his position, mewed in protest.

They both laughed, and Grace found herself smiling for the first time.

"Sorry, Socks," Yadira said, as they both stroked the miffed cat.

He settled down on Yadira's lap again with a warning glance to them both.

Lincoln got up, stretched, and trotted over.

"Good boy," Grace said, stroking him. He licked her, licked Yadira, and made a snuffing noise at Socks.

"He wants me to feel better," Grace said. Her dog's adoring look was comforting, and she hugged him. "Good boy," she repeated.

Lincoln jumped up on the couch beside her and she hugged him again.

"Things will look better tomorrow," Yadira predicted, patting Lincoln.

"I hope so," Grace repeated.

But things didn't look much better, Grace thought bleakly, as she sat at her desk and pulled a folder toward her.

She hadn't slept well that night. Arriving at work earlier than usual, she saw no sign of Brian. Tina was on the phone and Grace didn't want to ask her when he might be in.

She knew instinctively that Brian still needed time to sort things out in his mind. The incident with Victoria was still fresh, his nerves still raw, and he couldn't think logically. But after a day or two, she hoped the soreness would diminish. And he would be less emotional about the episode.

Then she could try speaking with him again.

An hour later, as she was finishing selecting some music for later in the week—and trying to stay away from melancholy songs that would only emphasize her mood—Grace heard Brian's voice. She'd left her door slightly ajar, and within a minute she heard his footsteps in the hall. The door of his office opened, and closed.

So he was not ready to talk yet.

Grace swallowed a lump of disappointment. Reaching for her handy water bottle, she quickly drank some. She wanted to sound fine when she went on the air.

Just give him some time, she told herself. *Like Yadira said, he'll come around, once he has time to think.*

If only she could feel as sure as her friend did.

Will was playing "Crystal Blue Persuasion" right now, and the song always reminded Grace of her sister. Maybe she'd give Crystal a call tonight.

She closed her eyes, willing herself to relax, to concentrate on the job she had to do. Forget about Brian right now, she told herself. Leave him alone for a day.

She went over, in her mind, some of the day's musical selections.

By the time she started her show, she was feeling a little better, and was able to focus on the music.

Halfway through a song by the Rolling Stones, she saw movement outside the studio. Glancing through the window, she saw Brian was heading toward the door, dressed in his coat, briefcase in hand.

He looked up and met her eyes.

His expression was guarded.

He paused, and gave her a stiff smile.

She tried to smile back, and waved.

He continued down the hall.

Well, at least it's something, she thought. At least he wasn't cutting off all lines of communication.

The song ended.

Grace leaned into the mike. "And that was the Rolling Stones with 'Jumpin' Jack Flash'," she said, making her voice as bright as she could. She was proud that she sounded normal. "And here's a word from Pizza Heaven. When we return, we'll hear a tune by the Grassroots."

She sat back again as the engineer cued the new commercial. It was nearly time for a news break, then her special show.

Tomorrow, she told herself, *things will get better.*

Brian sat in his favorite chair, the TV turned to the news channel. The microwave dinner on the snack table in front of him had lost its appeal before he'd eaten half of it, and the latest political scandal in the news seemed too stupid to merit any attention.

For the last twenty-four hours, he'd been consumed with confused thoughts.

There was Victoria and her betrayal. How dare she come into his office, thinking she could simply resume their relationship? He wouldn't get involved with her if he was paid millions. No, he knew full well that she was a fake, not to be trusted. She had totally lost her appeal.

And he was certain that even if he temporarily lost his sanity and went out with Victoria again, fell for her again, she'd end up dumping him the moment some other more powerful guy came along. No, he didn't trust her. And he definitely didn't want her.

He'd learned his lesson.

And now that he'd had that reminder of how devious women could be, of how fleeting love was, he was afraid he'd have to break off his relationship with Grace.

Thoughts of Grace made his heart tighten. He pictured her beautiful face. The last time they'd talked her eyes had been tearful.

And whose fault was that? he thought grimly. Not Victoria's.

He had let Grace fall in love with him, despite the fact that he didn't want to get involved. And now he was going to have to hurt her. Because when their relationship was over—which seemed imminent now, not far away—she would be hurt. Terribly. Grace was optimistic, believing in true love, and he didn't share that vision.

He shook his head, his heart feeling like it was being squeezed. Painfully.

It was better that he was stopping their relationship now, he told himself.

The TV switched to a recap of sports, and he tried to focus on the New Jersey Devils hockey team highlights they were showing. That lasted about a minute, and then Grace filled his mind again.

He should talk to her, he thought dully. Explain his feelings. He owed her that.

He stared at the phone.

But when he picked it up, he found himself calling his best friend, Joe.

Joe wasn't home. He hung up.

And continued to stare at the phone.

* * *

Tomorrow will be better, Grace repeated to herself as she got ready for bed.

She slid under the covers and switched off her night table lamp. "Good night, Lincoln," she whispered. Lincoln, already asleep on the old comforter in the corner, gave a doggy snore.

Sleep eluded Grace, despite her weariness. She kept going over the scene with Brian in her mind.

What, she wondered for the thousandth time, was going to happen now?

Should she just continue to give him space? Was he simply going to back away from their relationship without a second glance?

She thought about Victoria, and what she stood for. She'd reminded Bran of all the bad repercussions that could happen when you fell in love.

Well, Grace thought, maybe he needed to be reminded of the good things that could happen.

But how?

She turned on her side. What could she do to remind Brian that there was such a thing as true love? And that she felt it for him?

She could just march into his office and tell him.

She considered that for a few minutes. But somehow, the idea seemed flat and unconvincing.

She wanted to do something special, something that would get Brian's attention and really show him how she felt.

What could she do?

There were cards. But that idea seemed cliched. She could send him flowers. But that, too, had been done before. Sending an e-mail greeting seemed too small a gesture. She could try calling and singing to him—

Grace went still, as an idea exploded in her head.

She could tell him on the radio.

Now *that* would be unique. And distinctly the style of Grace Harmony Norwood.

Grace sat up in bed and switched on her lamp.

Lincoln blinked, stretched, and went back to dreamland.

Grace opened the drawer of the nightstand and found paper and a pen. She rapidly began to jot down ideas.

She wrote quickly, putting down a few phrases she might use, rejecting some, adding others.

And as she wrote, she had another notion; along with her little speech, she could play an appropriate song.

Now she began a list in earnest, writing down any song that might apply. She'd choose one tomorrow. As the list grew, she found herself growing more determined.

She would convince Brian. She *had* to.

A half-hour later, Grace turned off the light and pulled the comforter up to her chin. With a course of action planned, she felt much better. At least she had something to do besides sit around and feel sorry for herself.

This would work.

And if it didn't, she told herself, at least she had tried her best to open Brian's eyes. She hadn't just sat around, moping. She had taken action.

She snuggled into the pillow, picturing Brian's face the day they'd gone skiing. She would hold onto that image, not a more recent one.

Feeling more optimistic than she had all day, Grace drifted into sleep.

Brian was up early, despite the fact that he hadn't slept well. He was in the office before 9:00 at his desk with a mug of fresh coffee, organizing the items he had to take care of today.

And trying hard not to linger on thoughts of Grace. Or Victoria.

He had only two appointments this morning. He'd spent several hours last night catching up on paperwork, and once the appointments and any subsequent work was done, he'd have some free time today.

To do what? the little voice in his mind asked harshly.

Brian lifted his coffee mug and took a drink. The hot liquid, with only a trace of milk, slid down his throat. The aroma was rich and energizing. But it didn't warm him enough. He'd felt cold the last few days, and he knew it wasn't simply the weather.

He missed Grace.

He missed her smile. He missed her laugh. Her bright eyes. He missed her voice, talking to him.

Telling him she loved him.

He rested his chin on his hand. His heart was actually aching.

A bigger, deeper ache than he'd ever felt for Victoria.

Without Grace, his life had developed a gaping hole in it. Like a gigantic fissure in the earth.

It was like nothing he'd ever experienced before. Grace had gotten to him. Surrounded him with brightness and sunshine.

Filled his life with love and laughter.

And now those things were gone, leaving behind an empty void that only she could fill.

Compared to this wrenching emptiness, the pain he'd felt after Victoria's betrayal long ago seemed like a tiny pothole in the ground.

Was this love? This intense feeling he had for Grace? A feeling that nothing, and no one, could replace her?

It hadn't felt like that when he broke up with Victoria. He'd been hurt, and angry. But he hadn't felt like part of his soul was missing.

He needed to talk to someone, he thought desperately.

An email late last night from his buddy Joe had announced he was out of town on business for a couple of days.

Brian stared at the phone.

He could talk to Lois.

He grabbed the phone and dialed his sister's cell phone number.

Despite the fact that he was a few minutes early, Lois had already arrived at the restaurant where they'd agreed to meet for lunch.

"Thanks for meeting me at the last minute," Brian said, giving her a big hug.

"That's okay," Lois said, stepping back and surveying him with a critical look. They took their seats at the table, and her pensive look remained fastened on him. "I need a break from work. What's going on, Bri? I don't think I've ever heard you sound so—desperate." Her voice softened on the last word.

Brian sighed heavily, reaching for his water glass, and took a gulp. "I'll tell you. I need some sisterly advice."

"Hey, don't feel guilty. That's what big sisters are for." Lois gave him a smile. "So, tell me what's on your mind."

Brian proceeded to tell Lois the entire story of the last few days, pausing only when the waitress took their order and then brought them the soup of the day.

Lois listened intently as he spoke. When he finished telling her about his confused, painful feelings, he took a spoonful of the hot soup. The homemade chicken-and-noodle mixture was warm and soothing.

Lois put down her spoon and sat back, a thoughtful expression on her face.

"Well," she began, "believe it or not, my first thought as your were speaking was I'm glad Victoria showed up."

"What?" Brian stared at her.

"Because," she continued, "now you've seen her, from a different perspective, with the events of the past way behind you. You can see her for what she is—a money-hungry social climber. She's no good, and she never was! You're better off without her. You *know* that, Brian."

"That's true," he began, "but—"

"Wait. My thought was, now you can put that whole episode with Victoria behind you. And get on with your life."

Brian stared at Lois. "But I have gotten on with my life," he protested.

Lois shook her head. "Not completely, Brian. You're like I was for a long time, stuck on something that happened in the past, unable to move—emotionally—beyond what had happened."

Brian digested her words along with the comforting soup. Was Lois right?

"Remember how I told you about meeting Craig? I was stuck on the past, too, but he helped me overcome it, and see that it was time for me to move forward, and not dwell on past events. To move toward a new love. And I'm so happy, Brian."

Brian could feel the knot in his gut still twisting. "Maybe that's how things worked for you, Lois," he said. "But this is different."

"How?" she challenged.

"Because—" Brian stopped.

How . . . ? He was at a loss.

Lois had been hurt. She'd learned to trust again.

And he'd been hurt. But despite his intentions, Grace had gotten to him, gotten under his skin, with her everything-is-beautiful view of the world.

With her love.

And he knew then that he had guessed correctly when he'd wondered if he was in love.

His eyes met Lois's.

"Lois, I'm in love with her." He said it firmly, knowing with each word it was the absolute truth.

"Good for you." She gave him a wide grin.

"No," he said, "it's not good. I've hurt her. I didn't want to get too involved. I only wanted to be friendly. I know love isn't some everlasting, wonderful cure-all—"

"Not a cure-all, certainly," Lois responded crisply. "But it can be everlasting, and it certainly is wonderful. Do you want to know what my next thoughts were as you were telling me about Victoria and your discussion with Grace?"

"What?" he asked.

She smiled again. "Don't take this wrong, but I had an impulse to knock you on the head and say, 'get over it! Get real!' You've got to let go of the past with Victoria. This is *now,* Brian."

Lois had wanted to knock him on the head? He stared at his sister as she leaned toward him.

"Don't let your brooding on the past cause you to pass up your chance for true happiness," she continued calmly. "I almost did, and I'm so glad I didn't. Let it go, Brian, and move on."

"And what if it doesn't work?" he asked sharply.

Lois shrugged. "Nothing's guaranteed, of course, but if it doesn't, you'll be right back where you were before. Only more mature. If things work, though, Brian—and I think they can based on what I've seen of Grace—well, you have a great deal of happiness to look forward to. Don't forget, Brian, Grace is not Victoria. She's a kind, caring person."

Lois's words seeped through him, washing away some of his mixed feelings. But not all.

"Yes, Grace is kind and caring," he said. "But even if I decided you were right and took your advice, it may already be too late. I've told Grace our relationship probably should be cooled off, and I've hurt her—something I never intended to do."

"It's not too late." Lois shook her head vigorously. "Brian, don't take this wrong, either, but women—well, we're a little more flexible and forgiving than men. If you go to Grace and tell her how you're feeling, and that you want to try to work things out, I don't believe that she'd turn you away. I think she'd say she wants to try too."

Still Brian hesitated.

"She loves you," Lois said softly. "I think she'll forgive you for anything you said before and welcome you back."

"I don't know," Brian said with trepidation. "She was so hurt—"

"And now she'll be so happy," Lois repeated. "Do you really love her?"

"Yes," Brian said. "I love her." As he repeated the words, they reverberated in his brain. And his heart. He knew how true they were. "I love Grace."

Lois smiled. "I have a feeling you'll have your happy ending."

Could his sister be right? Brian pondered her words through lunch and all the way back to the office.

The worried part of him was afraid. *You're better off withdrawing from Grace, never getting into this love situation again,* it said.

But he *had* fallen in love, the other part of him argued. Without ever intending to, he'd given his heart to Grace.

He loved Grace. He was positive this feeling wouldn't change.

And he wanted her in his life.

He pulled into the radio station's parking lot, and turned off the car. And deliberately squelched the negative voice inside.

From now on, he'd listen only to the positive voice within.

Instead of getting out, he sat, reflecting on his sister's words. And his own feelings.

Had he ruined his chances with Grace? he wondered, feeling his stomach twist. Would she forgive him?

He needed time away from the office, to think about a course of action.

He pulled out of the lot and turned toward his home.

For the first time, Grace felt relief when she saw that Brian's Jeep wasn't in the parking lot at the radio station.

Before she saw him again, she wanted to put her plan into motion.

And before she did that, she owed it to Charles Armstrong to run her idea past him.

She hurried into the building and went to see Charles.

Chapter Ten

Grace sat in the studio, her heart beating rapidly. The news was almost finished, and then there'd be a commercial break, the weather forecast, and she'd be on the air.

She glanced out the window. The late afternoon was cold and gray, with occasional snowflakes meandering down from the sky. But despite the bleak sky, she felt warm with determination.

She was going to try to get to Brian. To prove how she felt and wake him up to reality.

Jan finished with news of a fire in the next town which had demolished a home, but from which the family and their pets had escaped. Grace listened as Jan read the list of places where contributions for the family could be sent. An advertisement for the All That Glitters jewelry store rolled, and Grace looked down at her speech. She practically had it memorized.

As the ad ended, she sipped some water from her water bottle, and listened to the weather forecast for the rest of the day and tomorrow morning.

". . . and now here's our station's favorite Flower Child, Grace Norwood!" Jan introduced her.

Grace leaned forward. "Hello, and welcome to an afternoon of classic hits for your listening pleasure," Grace said into the mike. "We'll begin with one of my personal favorites from the Young Rascals, 'Good Lovin'. And after that, we'll talk about that all-important topic : love!" Her voice sounded brighter than it had the day before.

As the music started, she sat back. She said a little prayer that Brian would be listening as he usually did. She was counting on it. But she'd already made plans in case he wasn't listening. Carl, the engineer, was taping her show.

As the song came to its exciting instrumental finish, Grace leaned forward again.

The moment the last note had died away, she spoke.

"Before I play the next song, there's something I have to say." She made her voice pleasant, but serious. "There's someone special out there who I hope is listening."

Grace hesitated, and took a long, calming breath. Her heart was beating a staccato rhythm. "I want the person I love to know I'll *never* stop loving him. Ever." She hadn't expected tears to well up in her eyes.

"You know who you are," she continued, more softly. "Please give our relationship a chance. Don't let a bad experience in the past rule your life."

She paused, then went on. "There's a song that explains it better than I possibly can. Listen to the words and the meaning. It's all true."

Without hesitation she cued the song.

"You ask me if there'll come a time . . ."

Grace blinked as the words and melody enveloped her.

Please be listening, Brian! Please open your heart and hear what I'm saying.

The mellow, sweet notes, harmonizing voices, and loving words of The Association's hit song continued.

". . . Never my love, never my love."

She pictured Brian's face the night of the hospital dance. And the day they'd gone skiing.

As the song reached its end, Grace thought about Charles's words when she'd left his office.

"Good luck, Grace. I think it will work." Charles had grinned. "And if it doesn't, Brian's a fool."

As the final notes faded, Grace cued up the next commercial without comment.

A movement by the inside window had her heart pounding. It was Charles. He was smiling, and he gave her a thumbs-up sign.

Grace smiled back shakily.

Brian stood by his living-room window, staring out at the snow-covered hill. Wind skimmed wisps of snow from the ground and tossed them in the air, mirroring the tossed-about feelings swirling through him. The radio, tuned to WQNJ, provided background music.

Why had he spent so much time brooding about Victoria? He must have been in kind of a state of shock for a while, he mused. But he had snapped out of it. And he felt very satisfied that he had finally told Victoria off. Now he really could get on with his life, as Lois said.

He had grown more sure with each passing moment that he loved Grace. And that he wanted her in his life.

Permanently. As in forever.

Lois was right. Victoria was out of his system and he could move on. He could take a chance on loving Grace.

Not such a big chance, he thought reflectively, if she loved him too.

But he'd hurt her terribly. Would she forgive him?

Or would she feel, as he once had, that she was better off without love?

But that didn't sound like Grace.

So the question was, how did he tell Grace that he loved her? That she had been right about love all along? And how did he make it up to her?

Picking up the phone seemed like a stupid way to tell someone you finally realized you loved them. No, he had to do better than that.

He picked up the note he'd found on his desk the other day, the note she'd written suggesting that Lewis and Joyce go out together.

He smiled. Who would have thought that a modern Flower Child would ever have gotten to him like this?

The news began, and Brian realized it was almost time for Grace to start her program. He dropped into his favorite chair, listening half-heartedly to the national news, followed by Jan with the local news, and tried to figure out what his next move should be.

Obviously, he couldn't contact Grace now. She was about to go on the air. It gave him some time to think and plan.

He heard her smooth, warm voice, and pictured her face as she'd looked the day they skied together, before Victoria had burst on the scene. He pictured Grace's brilliant eyes, her soft chocolate-colored hair, her loving smile.

If only she was sitting next to him now. He'd hold her tight and tell her exactly how he felt.

Grace said something about discussing love after the next song.

Bright notes filled the room, and Brian took a deep breath. Maybe he should meet her at the station. But they'd have no privacy there. Maybe at her home . . .

He thought of and rejected several scenarios.

He couldn't wait to see her. He was toying with the idea of meeting her as soon as her show was over, when he heard her voice on the air again.

Brian listened to Grace, her voice more serious than usual. He stared at the radio as she expressed the hope that someone special was listening to her show.

Suddenly, Brian's heart started to thud.

"I want the person I love to know I'll *never* stop loving him. Ever."

He inhaled sharply at Grace's words, his body tensing as she continued to speak.

She asked for time to give a relationship a chance to grow. *Me!* he thought. *She's talking about me!*

Brian sat upright.

There was a slight pause, and Grace went on as Brian sat, his heart hammering. "There's a song that explains it better than I possibly can. Listen to the words and the meaning. It's all true."

Seconds later he heard the soft strains of romantic music, and the beautiful lyrics.

He squeezed his eyes shut, more touched than he'd ever been in his life.

She loved him. Grace still loved him!

Opening his eyes, the room looked the same—but it was different. Suddenly the room, his home, the whole universe was full of light and happiness.

His heart was speeding away as he listened to the words of the song. He jumped up. He *had* to see Grace!

The moment the notes of the song faded away, he grabbed his coat.

His personal Flower Child was a true romantic.

Which required a romantic response!

And a plan began to formulate in the corners of his mind as he practically raced to his car.

Grace was anxious all through her broadcast, moving on her seat, drumming her fingers while music played. She found herself hardly able to have a quick snack during the long news break. Everytime she heard a phone ring in the distance, she jumped.

Would he call? Would he come in?

Had Brian even been listening to the radio? What if he hadn't heard her?

Grace knew Brian usually kept their station on all the time. But suppose he wasn't listening—suppose he was skiing, or in the shower, or out of the area when she was on?

And the worst alternative—one she could barely stand to consider—what if he didn't want to speak to her? What if her plea hadn't moved him at all?

She couldn't believe he'd be so cold-hearted as to ignore her romantic gesture. Even if he didn't change his mind, surely he would talk to her about what she'd said.

Wouldn't he?

By the end of her broadcast, Grace was becoming tired. There were no messages for her when she went back to her desk. Discouraged, she gathered her things, and drove home.

Lincoln bounded over when she entered the house, and she dropped her purse and kneeled down to hug her dog.

"Good boy, good boy," she said, hugging him fiercely. Lincoln licked her face.

The livingroom lights were all on, the room bright and inviting. Yadira looked up from the romance novel she was reading. "Hi. How are you?"

"Okay," Grace said. "Was Lincoln out recently?"

"Yeah, but—"

The dog, hearing the suggestion, jumped up.

"Okay, okay," Grace said, trying to smile. "Let's go out."

"I heard you on the radio," Yadira said, her tone warm and sympathetic.

Grace blinked, sudden tears pricking at her eyes. "Did I sound incredibly stupid?"

"No, you sounded like a woman in love. Want some hot cocoa?"

It was just what she needed. "Okay," Grace said, "as soon as I get back."

She went out into the backyard with Lincoln, letting the dog cavort in the snow, petting him as he returned to her. As he shook himself, snow sprinkled all over her. It felt good against her warm cheeks.

She returned inside, shed her coat, and gave Lincoln a milkbone. He dashed off to eat it in his favorite corner of the living room. Socks appeared from behind her, and she handed him a cat treat, which he took delicately, marching back to a shadowy corner of the kitchen.

Yadira had turned the radio on to WQNJ, and Grace noticed as she kicked off her shoes that the volume was unusually loud.

"Here," Yadira said. She handed Grace a mug and Grace took it gratefully, sinking down into one of the chairs in the room.

"Tell me everything," Yadira said, returning to the couch. Socks reappeared and sprang up to curl into Yadira's lap.

Grace told Yadira about her idea, the song she'd chosen, and getting Charles' approval. "I'm sure he suspected all along how I felt," she added. "But he didn't say anything, just acted glad to help."

She noticed as she spoke that Yadira glanced at the radio several times. She knew her friend well, and it almost seemed that she was waiting for something.

"Have you heard anything from Brian?" Yadira asked.

Once again Grace felt close to tears. "No. Not a word. What if he wasn't listening, Yadira? What if he doesn't care?" Doubts crowded in.

"I'm sure he cares," Yadira said quickly. "I've seen the way he looks at you. Of course, he might not have been listening— but doesn't he usually? Don't all of you usually listen to your station?"

"Yes, but—what if he was watching TV or in the shower—"

The song on the radio ended, and Grace heard Charles's voice. Surprised, she turned in the direction of the radio. Charles rarely went on the air, unless it was for a fundraiser, or some kind of emergency—

". . . and now we have a change of programming," he said cheerfully. "We're departing from our usual format to bring you a special message."

Grace stared at the radio.

"As you know, Valentine's Day is only two days away. Right now we have a special message from our own Brian Talbot."

Grace's heart began to hammer, and her hands trembled. She had to put down her mug of cocoa. She wrapped her arms around her body, waiting . . . hoping.

"Our listeners know that we've been running a Valentine's promotion during the last few weeks." The timbre of Brian's voice was deep and warm. "The object has been to find a date for me, and for our DJ, Grace Norwood."

He paused for a second. "I've chosen from our listening audience three women to date, and I'm supposed to chose my Valentine's date from among them." Again he hesitated briefly.

"I've chosen my date," Brian said slowly. "And although the three women I previously dated were all very special in their own ways, and would make wonderful dates for Valentine's Day, it's not any of them."

Grace met Yadira's eyes. Yadira was grinning broadly.

Grace's heart was beating so loud she thought Yadira could hear it. She could scarcely breathe, anxiously straining to hear what Brian would say next.

"It wouldn't be fair to take them out when I've fallen in love. The woman I want to spend Valentine's Day with is the only woman in the world for me. The woman I love. Grace Norwood."

Sunshine burst through Grace, and she could have sworn she heard fireworks.

Brian loved her! He loved *her*!

She was trembling all over now, as Brian went on. "Grace, I've been doing a lot of thinking, and I heard your message on the radio. I hope you feel exactly the way I do. There's no one else I want to spend Valentine's Day with."

Grace felt tears in her eyes as her heart soared. She met Yadira's look and bounced up, running to give her friend a gigantic hug.

Music started, and Grace heard the notes of a song she hadn't heard for a while. Donna Summer sang "On the Radio."

"He loves me," she declared jubilantly. "He loves me!" All the while she was listening to the Donna Summer song. The words had taken on a new meaning.

"That's right," Yadira said.

"You knew, didn't you?" Grace asked.

"Brian called just before you got off the air. He said he'd cooked up something with Charles's help, and I was to make sure the radio was on when you got home."

"I have to see him!" Grace catapulted off the couch. Lincoln got up, looking at her quizzically. Even Socks stared.

"Wait." Yadira held up her hand. "I have strict orders not to let you go anywhere right now."

Delight shot through her. "He's coming *here?*"

"That's right," Yadira said.

"I—oh, I better get ready!" Grace exclaimed.

She had never been so excited. She ran into her bedroom, turned on the radio there, and grabbed a brush, quickly stroking it through her hair. All the time her heart was singing to the tune on the radio, as her mind repeated, *He loves me! He loves me!* and Donna Summer crooned "On the Radio."

Grace was ready in less than five minutes. She paced from her room to the living room and back while Yadira and Lincoln and Socks watched her. After a minute, Socks decided nothing spectacular was going on and dozed off. Lincoln sat down and continued to regard her.

"I think I'll make myself scarce," Yadira said, laughing. "Good luck."

Grace reached out and hugged her friend again. "Thanks, and thanks for all your help."

"You go, girl," Yadira said.

"It will probably take him at least fifteen minutes to get here," Grace said.

He made it in twelve. Grace heard the car pull into the driveway and flew to the door.

She waited until his footsteps were coming up the walk and then flung the door open.

"Brian!" She flew out the door and ran down the walk.

Brian ran the last few yards to meet her.

"Grace!" He scooped her up and held her tightly against him as their lips met in a sizzling kiss.

Grace felt the kiss through her entire being, right down to her toes.

Brian pulled back. "You're going to freeze out here."

"Not when you kiss me like that." She met his dazzling

smile with one of her own. "Oh, Brian, I heard you on the air—"

"And I heard you too." Brian carried her inside, depositing her in the livingroom, and firmly shut the door. Grace met the loving look in his hazel eyes, and another thrill of pure happiness flowed through her.

"Grace." Brian's expression turned serious, and he pulled her toward the couch, and sat down close to her, shedding his coat. "I owe you an apology. When I saw Victoria, it did something to me. Set off bad memories, and shook me up. I wasn't thinking clearly, I was just acting with old bottled-up anger. I should never have taken it out on you."

"It's all right—" she began.

"No. Wait." Brian put a finger to her lips, then caressed her cheek gently. His voice was unsteady as he spoke. "All I can say is, I'm sorry. I should never have reacted that way. I should have realized immediately that you're a much better person than Victoria could ever be, and that you'd never act like her. I should have trusted you."

His heartfelt words brought more tears to her eyes.

"Before I even heard you on the radio," he continued, moving to clasp Grace's hands, "I had done some real hard thinking. I realized I loved you and didn't want the past to spoil what we had together. And I was wondering if you'd let me back into your life." He smiled. "Then I heard you, and heard the song, and knew I still had a chance." He squeezed her hands. "I love you, Grace Harmony."

"Oh, Brian," she whispered. "I love you too."

He pulled her into his arms and captured her lips with his.

Grace was dizzy with happiness. When he finally let her go, he was smiling at her, and she knew she wore an identical, loving smile on her face.

"My own Flower Child," he whispered, and pulled her tightly against him. Burying his face in her hair, Brian whispered, "I finally found somebody to love."

Epilogue

"The limo's here," Yadira announced, peeking into Grace's room.

Grace took one last look in the mirror. "Thanks." She was wearing her burgundy dress, the one Brian had admired at the hospital dance, for their Valentine's Day date, and had pinned on it the corsage Brian had sent ahead of time. Her eyes shone as she checked her makeup in the glass.

A knock on the door started Lincoln barking, and Grace followed Yadira to the door, which she opened.

Brian stood outside, dressed in a black tux, looking incredibly handsome. His eyes lit up as he took a look at her. "You look beautiful," he said simply.

Grace felt a tremor go through her. "Thank you. And you look so handsome."

Brian took her coat and helped her on with it. Grace felt small and feminine beside him. He offered her his arm and said gallantly, "Shall we go?"

They waved as Yadira told them to have fun and shut the door behind them.

The limo was long and classy, and as soon as it started down the street, Brian took the champagne which was chilling in a bucket and poured them each a glass.

"How elegant!" Grace said, accepting the glass. "Are Lewis and Joyce meeting us at the restaurant?"

"Yes, the other limo's picking them up. We have separate tables though."

"So they'll get a chance to get to know each other," Grace said happily, sipping the bubbly liquid.

"Not only that. We'll be celebrating," Brian said mysteriously.

"Celebrating . . . falling in love?" Grace asked.

"Yes, and celebrating my coming to my senses," Brian continued. "And . . ."

"And?" Grace probed.

His smile was slightly mischievous. "Wait a few minutes. You'll see."

They spent the next few minutes cuddling and sipping their champagne. Grace felt incredibly happy, and Brian's shining eyes and smile told her he felt the same.

The limo rolled to a stop. "This is our first stop," Brian announced. "A small detour on the way to the restaurant."

Puzzled, Grace looked at him, then peered out the window.

They were parked in front of the local jewelry store, All That Glitters.

Her heart flew into her throat. She couldn't voice the hope that suddenly engulfed her. "Brian? . . ."

He turned her to face him, and now his face wore a serious expression. "Grace," he said, taking her hands in his. "I love you. I not only found somebody to love—I found the most wonderful *somebody* I could ever hope to find. You're the only woman for me."

She could hardly breathe.

He brought her hands to his lips and kissed them softly. "I want you to always be my love. Permanently. I want to spend *every* Valentine's Day with you."

Grace's heart was jumping up and down.

"Will you marry me?" he asked simply, his eyes holding hers.

"Yes, oh yes," she answered, and flung her arms around his neck.

Their lips met and clung. Grace had never felt so ecstatic.

"Grace, Grace, I love you," he whispered, kissing her over and over.

"I love you, Brian!" she exclaimed, returning each kiss enthusiastically.

When they pulled apart, totally breathless from the intensity of their kisses, Brian was grinning. "Come on. Let's pick out your engagement ring. I want the whole world to know you're mine."

"I love you," Grace whispered.

Brian gave her an adoring look. "I love you. Now we'll both have somebody to love . . . forever."